LORI'S REDEMPTION

by

Pamela S Thibodeaux

LORI'S REDEMPTION
By: Pamela S. Thibodeaux
Copyright © 2012

Publisher/Distributor:
Temperance Publishing, an imprint of
Pamela S Thibodeaux Enterprises, LLC
PO Box 324, Iowa, LA 70647

ISBN: 978-1-7353393-4-4

Cover Design:
Delia Latham; Heaven's Touch Designs

Dedication

All ***Thanks*** belong to God for the glorious gift He has entrusted me with – the gift of writing that enables me to share my faith and His love with the world!

To Donna, critique partner and friend – Thanks for ***ALL*** you do!

For all the cowboy preachers out there – May God Bless the work you do.

Special ***Thanks*** to all of the authors, writers, poets and artists who have paved the way for me to do what I love and whose work I admire – ***Thank you, Thank You, Thank you!***

And last but not least, ***THANK YOU***, dear reader! I pray you've been blessed as I have by your purchase of this book. If you've enjoyed ***Lori's Redemption*** please write a positive review and post it at online retailers (Amazon, B&N, Kobo, iBooks, etc.) and websites where readers gather and/or your social media platforms (FaceBook, Good Reads, BookBub, Twitter, etc).

Praise for Pamela S Thibodeaux

"Pamela Thibodeaux uses her masterful story writing art to create a powerful story of how God heals a woman's heart —broken by grief— through recovery, love and triumph." ~ CBA Best-Selling Author DiAnn Mills on **My Heart Weeps**.

"A great collection of short stories. Each one includes inspirational romance. Wonderful choice when you need a quick pick-me-up. I have not been one to read short stories. This book has changed that. There are times when they are the perfect choice." ~ (Amazon) Review of **Love in Season** by K. Neely

"Loved this book. Wish everyone could read this. Definitely puts all holidays in perspective. If we remember the reason for the holidays then we must put God first.......always. I will certainly recommend this book. Great stuff keep up the great writing." ~ (Amazon) Review of **Keri's Christmas Wish** by Reba

"Oh, the passion, faith and just LIFE that flows through this book...powerful writing indeed!" ~ Review of **Circles of Fate** by Deena Peterson, Book Reviewer @ A Peek at my Bookshelf and Just One More

"Thibodeaux leads the reader through from the first page to the last without once relinquishing control. She hooks them, holds them, and keeps them enthralled until the last line." ~ Review of **The Visionary** by Delia Latham

*"**In His Sight** caught my attention from the beginning and it made me wonder if I had given all to God as he gave all to me. Thank you, Pamela for a story that I would readily recommend to anyone who needs that extra encouragement!"* ~ Reviewed by Wendy for Happily Ever After Reviews.

*"**Winter Madness** is a wonderful romance and an excellent example of Spiritual growth."* ~Reviewed by Dee Daily for The Romance Studio

*"**A Hero for Jessica is** a good, sweet read charged with attraction but an emphasis on true love. I recommend it to women of all ages."* ~ Reviewed by Violet for LASR

*"**Cathy's Angel** is a short tale that is entertaining as well as inspiring. Well done!"* ~ Reviewed by Marlene for Fallen Angel Reviews

*"Pamela S. Thibodeaux's motto is "Inspirational with an Edge!" Her short story **Choices** lives up to*

those words and is well worth reading." ~Reviewed by *Gail for Night Owl Romance*

*"**The Inheritance** was my first Thibodeaux work; however, it will not be my last! Her approach to writing about everyday life, while struggling to maintain strict Christian standards and values, is a glimpse into reality which we all must face from time to time."* ~ Reviewed by Brenda Talley for The Romance Studio

*"If you have ever considered Christian fiction bland, then check out the **Tempered Series**. It will be well worth your time."* ~ Amanda Killgore ~ for Huntress Reviews.

Chapter One

Eager for fresh air, Lori Strickland pulled on her tights, shorts, and slid leg warmers over her calves. A hooded sweatshirt covered her tank top. Thick socks and tennis shoes completed her outfit, and she left her bedroom ready for her morning run. She slipped out the door, careful not to wake her parents feeling safe in knowing ranch hands would be stirring about and watch out for her as she traipsed the perimeters of her home. She stretched then started out at a slow jog then picked up her pace to match the whirlwind of her thoughts.

Through all the years of strife and turmoil, those tumultuous teenage years, running remained the one consistency in her life. Probably because it mirrored her desire to get away from the repressive atmosphere of small town existence. There wasn't much to do in Bandera, Texas. Nothing she hadn't done hundreds, maybe thousands of times already. Lori hated it, loathed every moment of being stuck in the rut of her reality.

High school was a drag. The day she graduated, a year behind her peers, she took off to work in various low-paying, dead-end jobs in San Antonio, hoping the big city would add spice to her life. Unable to support herself or survive without financial help from her father, she succumbed to his pressure and enrolled in community college then moved back home. Now, two years later she still had no degree, no real job, and no clue what to do with her life.

So glad its Saturday; no school today. Relief swept through her. Lori eased her frantic stride into a much smoother gait and took slow, deep breaths that heaved out in wisps of fog in the chilly air. She rolled her head and shoulders in an attempt to shake off the tension which built and crested with her thoughts. and took in the sights, smells, and sounds around her.

The rich, damp earth tickled her nostrils. A hint of spring teased her senses, its fullness and warmth only a few weeks away. Soon she'd be able to forego the tights, legwarmers, and sweatshirt for her customary shorts and tank or sleeveless t-shirt. Roosters crowed and horses neighed their welcome, night creatures scurried into nests and dens.

Before long, more than ranch hands would be out and about. Traffic would increase as people made their way to work or family outings. This was her favorite time of day, when night gave way to morning.

Lori slowed her pace as the sun peeked over the horizon and turned the sky into a masterpiece of contrast. Light and color battled the darkness, a hint of yellow, a burst of pink then peach, and finally orange.

Lori didn't think of herself as a spiritual person. Oh, she attended church, twice on Sunday and again on Wednesday as she had all of her life but found the routine stifling. But in this slice of time when darkness gave way to radiance and shadows turned from possibilities into reality, her spirit soared, and she hoped one day God would shed some light on His purpose for her life.

A ray of sunshine glinted off an object and caught the corner of her eye. Lori turned to her right and stared out over the arena where barrels sat, aligned in a perfect V-shape. A thought sparked. *Rodeo.*

She began to jog again then run. Her heartbeat quickened then thundered with excitement while the idea grew. As a child she loved to ride and compete in the annual charity rodeo hosted by the Rockin' H Ranch. When she entered high school, her social life replaced rodeo and barrels took a back seat to boys. Now in the dawn of a new day, the more she thought about the the possibilities rodeo may offer, the more excited she became. Riding the rodeo circuit just might be her ticket out of here! It would certainly be an outlet for the wanderlust that plagued her soul.

She'd have to start out as an amateur of course and work her way up to the pros, if possible.

All things are possible to them that believe.

Her spirit quickened. *Is that You, God? Are You showing me Your purpose for my life?*

She slowed again from a run to jog then walk and took several deep breaths to ease the thud of her heart. She stretched and listened for another word from God, but all she heard was the quiet whisper of her soul. *Rodeo.*

She hurried back in the house to find her parents seated at the breakfast table, coffee and newspaper in hand and greeted them both with a hug. "Hey, folks! Beautiful morning, isn't it?"

Her father peered over his section of the newspaper and eyed her with suspicion. "What's got you so all fired up this morning, besides your run?"

Lori laughed and hugged him again. The aroma of fresh-brewed coffee teased her nostrils, made her mouth water. She walked over to the counter and poured herself a cup. "Think I've finally figured out what God wants me to do with my life."

The statement garnered their undivided attention. Both laid the paper down and waited to hear what she had to say.

"I've searched high and low for the perfect career. I've even prayed for God to show me some kind of sign. I believe I received that sign this morning. I'm hitting the rodeo circuit."

"What makes you think that's God's plan?" Her father asked.

"The way the sun glinted off a barrel, the quickening of my spirit when I prayed, the calm assurance I feel now."

"Never realized you did much in the way of praying."

"Never been much for praying but had to get answers somehow. I can't stay stuck here with no purpose and no future. I need to *do* something with my life."

Her mother rose, picked up her coffee cup and poured the remains in the sink. "Well, what do you think you'll accomplish on the rodeo circuit? I never hear much good coming out of that. Only shattered bones for the riders and broken hearts for those who love them."

Lori sighed and rolled her eyes. "Oh, Mom, you always see the negative side of things. I've finally made a decision that may prove to be fruitful. Why can't you just be happy for me?"

"Just because I'm practical, doesn't mean I see the negative side of things, honey. I am happy for you if this is truly what you want and not just another way to run from life in a small town."

A flush heated her neck when Lori realized her mother knew her better than she'd imagined. Her mother smiled and ran a hand over her head, then cupped her cheeks in warm, gentle hands.

"I value your happiness above all things, Lori. If this is what you desire, your father and I will support you. If it turns out to be less than what you expect, you can always come home and consider other options. You're still young enough to try different things until you find your place in life."

"Thanks, Mom," she whispered.

"Now, how about a bite of breakfast?"

"That would be great. I'll take a quick shower and then I need to give Stanley a call. I bet he has the perfect, champion barrel racer for me."

Her father snorted. "I do own a ranch you know. We have champion horses here, too."

Lori laughed and bent to rub her nose against his in their favored childhood gesture. "Sure you do, Daddy, but Stanley's horses are proven champions. Since you raise and sell ranch horses, I think I'd prefer one of his."

"Humph, had I known the boy would put me out of business, I'd have sent him packing from this county ten years ago. Instead, like a fool, I hired him then turned him loose when he set up his own ranch."

Laughter bubbled out of Lori at the familiar joke. She straightened and turned on her heel, then tossed a comment over her shoulder. "Oh, please, tell that to someone who doesn't know better."

Her parents loved Stanley Morrison as the son they never had, for which she harbored no jealousy. He'd proven himself a worthy friend and as close as any flesh and blood brother could be.

She hurried into the shower but didn't linger in her normal fashion under the hot, pulsating water. Instead, she rushed through her routine, dressed and braided her hair. She wolfed down breakfast and all but slung dishes into the dishwasher. Afterward, she whizzed through her morning chores then slammed out of the house. She climbed into her truck, turned the radio to blaring, tore out of the drive, and hastened over to the Swinging M ranch, only to find the place deserted.

She hissed out a frustrated oath and berated herself for not calling first. She stormed out of the truck, stomped up on the porch and left a note on the pad attached to the door frame.

Need a barrel horse. Call me. Lori

She arrived home, walked to the pasture, gazed out over the barrels and envisioned herself speeding around them on a powerful animal. One built for speed and beauty. She climbed the fence and took off at a slow jog around the barrels, felt the thrill of success zing through her veins. Another confirmation. Less than an hour later her cell phone rang.

"Hey, Lors, what's up?"

"I need a horse, Stanley. A barrel horse. Got anything for me?"

"Matter of fact I do, a sorrel gelding, just under three years old. Often wondered why I hadn't been able to sell him before now. Kicked myself a time or two for having him cut so young when I could have studded him out. Guess he's meant for you."

Lori chuckled. A deeply spiritual man, Stanley always saw the big picture, knew there was a purpose for all things – good or bad. "When can I come and get him?"

"Anytime you're ready, or I can bring him over in a bit."

"That'd be great, Stan. We haven't seen you in a while and I know mom and dad would love to visit with you."

"Yeah, well I haven't gone far with Amber so close to delivering that boy of mine. Ours, he amended with a chuckle."

Lori laughed. "Amber must have cut you a pair of eyes for you to correct yourself so quick."

Stan chuckled. "You know us too well."

She giggled. "Tell Amber I won't keep you long. Just enough time to introduce me to the horse. What's his name anyway?"

"Solomon."

She gasped. *Conformation number three.* "I like that, Stan. So, we'll see you in a while?"

He assured her he'd be over with the horse shortly and they rang off. Excitement shivered through her and for the first time in a long time, Lori bowed her head outside of the church building.

"Lord, I'm not sure if all this is from You or not but thank You. I haven't felt this good, this excited about anything in my life for a while now. Like, forever, and I'm grateful. Help me to succeed."

She heard the rattle of truck and trailer and turned as Stanley pulled up to the barn and disembarked from his vehicle. She shouted and waved then ran over to meet him while he unloaded the horse. Her heart leapt into her throat when the huge sorrel backed out of the trailer with a snort and a toss of his perfectly-shaped head. Excitement curled through her, but she approached with caution.

He stood a full head and shoulders over her at the withers. She reached a tentative hand toward his muzzle, surprised when he sniffed then blew into her palm. In one quick movement, he shoved Stanley out of the way and leaned his head over her shoulder then pressed in until she wrapped her arms around his neck. The bond between them sealed in that moment. A primitive, sacred bond shared by horse and rider for centuries. Stanley's low wolf-whistle interrupted the moment.

"Wow, looks like I was right, he is meant for you. Seldom see a horse and rider connect so completely from the onset."

Lori buried her face in Solomon's neck and inhaled the heady scent of horseflesh then ran her fingers through his thick mane. "How much, Stan? I'll get daddy to write you a check."

His eyes narrowed into tiny blue flames. "Don't be ridiculous. He's a gift."

"But..."

Stan shook his head, effectively cutting off the remainder of her protest. "No buts about it and I don't want to hear another word."

She flung herself in his arms. "Thank you! Is he broke?"

Stan chuckled. "Green broke. He's had a saddle and rider a time or two. Run through his paces regularly but hasn't been around the barrels so you'll have to take it easy on him to start. But he's a champion and he's fast. He's cut young and cut proud, so he's spirited too. You'll need be careful, get to know him and let him get to know you before you put too much stress on his training."

"Will you help me train him?"

He nodded. "Much as I can with everything else going on with Amber, the twins and this son of mine on the way."

She laughed. "You keep saying it's a boy but I thought y'all didn't ask to know the sex."

He grinned. "We didn't. I just know."

"What if the baby turns out to be a girl?"

His eyes narrowed again but this time glittered with mirth. "Bite your tongue. I need another man around the house to balance things out. Even if it is a boy, we'll still be outnumbered."

"Only fair considering Amber has put up with you, her father and her brother all by herself since her mother's death." She gasped when sadness clouded his eyes. "I'm sorry, Stan. I didn't mean to sound so nonchalant."

He raked a hand over his face. "You didn't, Lors. The pain lessens with time but there are still days when the hole in our hearts and lives seems to gape open like a raw wound."

For lack of words Lori slid her arms around his waist and hugged him close. A sharp whistle garnered their attention. They turned toward the porch where her father waved them over. Glad for the diversion from the tense emotions that invaded the joyous moments, Stanley handed her the lead rope and they walked to meet him. He bolted off the porch and embraced Stanley in something between a headlock and bear hug.

"Stanley, my boy! How are you? No baby yet?"

Stan laughed. "Wonderful, Roy. No baby yet. He's not due for another month or so."

Roy released him and turned to examine the horse. "So, this is the champion barrel racer you've brought my daughter?" He ran a hand over the animal in an appreciative gesture. "How much do we owe you?"

Lori giggled when Stan shook his head with a sigh and mumbled, "Like father, like daughter. He's a gift." He smiled and held up a hand before Roy could say another word. "No arguments from you either. It'd be like charging my own father or sister for a horse."

"Yeah, well you've got to make a living."

"I do. A darn good one, thanks in part to you. Don't look a gift horse in the mouth."

Lori laughed when a frown creased her father's brow, but he bit his lip. She hugged Stanley again and clucked her tongue. "Come on, Solomon. I'll show you your new home."

She turned and led the horse away.

Solomon's training began the day after his arrival. In the years Lori had known Stan and watched him work, she understood the most important step in training a horse was for the animal to become familiar with its rider and home. She decided one of the quickest, easiest ways to accomplish that would be for Solomon to accompany her on her morning run.

Every day that first week, she held onto his lead rope and chatted with him while she jogged. When the need for speed kicked in, she turned him loose and they ran together. Once or twice, she had to call him back to her side when he wandered off to explore on his own. He returned without fuss or resistance. In the afternoons, she saddled him up and they rode over the same terrain they traversed each morning and ended with a walk or trot around the barrels. Before long he chomped at the bit to run.

The first few times she gave him his head, he bolted around the barrels in such a jerky, unsteady stride she had to hang on for dear life. Soon though, his gait lengthened and smoothed and the speed for which he'd been bred asserted itself and she knew she had a champion on her hands.

Chapter Two

Rafe Judson prepared to ride the killer bull despite the still, small voice in his head that urged him to walk away. The voice nagged him for weeks, said his age and health were strikes against his winning another title and urged him to quit while still ahead. Though mere whispers, the words screamed deep inside his heart. He knew whose voice echoed in his spirit and still tuned a deaf ear as he had when God first spoke.

I want no part of You, You took my mother from me, and I'll never forgive You.

His boots, scuffed and scarred from years of use, slid on his feet with ease. He caressed the worn leather with a soft cloth and wished, yet again, for someone to touch him with the same gentle care his mother had showered on him before each rodeo.

Ten years and he still missed her. Ten years and he still ignored her plea to never get on a killer bull. In his teenage years she supported his rodeo dreams - as long as he stuck to roping and broncos. The first time he mentioned bulls, she freaked. Still, he focused on that desire and practiced until he turned eighteen. With a great deal of reluctance, she accepted his decision to ride but begged him to be careful. She wrung a promise that he would walk away if the bull he drew turned out to be a killer.

He buried that promise the same day he buried her and never looked back.

He had no idea when God's voice replaced that of his mother, nor did he care. Bull riding was his passion, his calling. He'd never give it up. He'd die first.

Be careful what you say.

Fear curled through him, tightened like a fist in his gut. He squashed the feeling with ruthless determination. If I die, I die. We all die.

He buckled his spurs, tied his chaps and made his way from the ritzy travel trailer to the arena.

The voices in his head intensified with every step then multiplied until words jumbled, at war with one another. Some urged him not to ride. Others taunted, challenged him to just get on with it, mount the bull and leave the rest up to fate.

A stranger's voice joined in the fray. Rafe ignored him and, in a last-ditch effort to shut them all out, he climbed the fence and lowered himself onto the fifteen-hundred-pound animal without his usual pre-ride preparation. No mental exercise, no sweet talking the bull, nothing.

The bull balked and threw his head back with a belligerent snort. The horn missed Rafe's face by a hairsbreadth. His heart thundered. Bile rose in his throat. Rafe swallowed hard and shoved his hand into the rigging then wrapped the rope around and around, all the while knowing he should just climb off the bull and walk away.

The buzzer sounded, the gate swung open and the crowd roared to its feet as he clung to the hulk of madness between his thighs. Spurs bit into flesh. The bull grunted, snorting angry huffs of air through his nostrils, and bucked and twisted in an attempt to shake him off. Adrenaline pumped through Rafe as the seconds ticked by. Suddenly everything went wrong. His shoulder snapped, arm twisted, and in the process, flung him from his seat. He flopped around on the bull's back then slid beneath his belly.

Visions of death danced before his eyes as he dodged hooves. Voices clamored in his head. Fear raced through him. Blood sang in his ears.

Whether moments or an eternity, he had no idea how long he clung to the animal before the world went black.

Chapter Three

Her face tense, eyes focused, Lori leaned in the saddle and urged her mount into a full gallop around the barrels.

"How'd we do?" she asked Stanley, as she brought the horse to a sliding halt along the fence.

Stanley glanced at the stopwatch and smiled. "Better every day, Lors, down from 20.5 seconds to 19.0 in less than a month."

She slung down out of the saddle. "19.0 will never win, Stanley."

"Patience, Lori, he's young yet and you're still rusty from not competing in so long. Cool him down now and we'll talk."

He waited and watched while she walked the horse in circles around the arena. When she finished and headed toward the barn to unsaddle and groom, he followed. He reached for the brush and currycomb while she removed the saddle and blanket from the animal and set them on a shelf.

"Want to tell me what's wrong?"

The scowl she sent him spoke volumes. "What makes you think there's something wrong?"

He smiled over the horse's back and tossed her the brush. "Unhappiness is written all over your face, that's what."

"I just want to win, that's all. First the charity rodeo here and then I want to travel and ride."

Stanley eyed her with more than a hint of curiosity and concern. "What's so important about winning now, Lors when it wasn't a big deal five years ago?"

"I just want to be somebody, Stan, other than Roy Strickland's daughter and I want to make something of myself. I have no idea what yet, so this seems like a good way to focus my energy until I decide."

"No luck in college?"

She snorted. "College sucks. Besides, you know how much I hated school."

He couldn't help but chuckle. "That's true, barely graduated much to the dismay of your parents. No luck in finding Mr. Right either?"

Again, she snorted. "Around here? Not a chance."

Done with the grooming, they fed and watered the horse and walked out of the barn. "I'm afraid if you think riding the rodeo circuit will help out in that area, you're going to be sadly mistaken," he said.

Loir chafed at the subtle warning in his tone. "Just train Solomon and me so we can win and let me worry about my love life."

"Solomon will be fine. Just practice every day but don't stress or strain him. As for you, once upon a time I'd have bet my bottom dollar that you'd never make a champion horsewoman. Not anymore, you've come a long way from the gangly, unstable rider you were ten, even five years ago. But you still need to relax in the saddle. He knows what he's doing so just lean in and flow with your horse instead of trying to control every movement he makes."

Three weeks later she met Stanley and his wife outside the paddock at the charity rodeo hosted by the Rockin' H ranch.

Lori flung herself into his arms. "We did it, Stanley! We did it!"

"You did it, Lors, you won *All Around* Cowgirl."

"I couldn't have done it without you. You're still the best." She hugged him again then turned to Amber. "If you ever want to throw him out, give me a call. I'll take him off your hands."

Amber laughed and hugged her.

"Not a chance. Congratulations, Lori. Stanley's told me how hard you've worked, looks like it's paid off. What next?"

"On to bigger and better things, more titles and lots of cash," Lori said. "I've joined the Amateur Rodeo Association on both the state and national level.

Stanley frowned. "Why amateur?"

She looked at him as though he'd lost his mind. "I'm not a pro am I? I've got to start somewhere."

"You ought to get back in school and on the college team and circuit."

She narrowed her eyes and snorted. "You sound just like my father. I already told you college sucks, I don't want to go to back."

Stanley chuckled. "Whatever, Lors, I didn't come out to scold, only to congratulate you. Just remember what I've taught you, relax and flow with your horse and go easy on him."

She beamed. "I will, Stanley.

Chapter Four

Rafe opened his eyes then shut them with a moan. Pain sliced through his skull at the invasion of light in his pupils. A voice above him encouraged him to try again. He took a deep breath, steeled himself against the onslaught and peeked through lowered lids until his eyes adjusted. When open fully, he took in his surroundings and the unfamiliar face above him. Questions rolled around in his head. He moved his mouth to speak but no words came forth.

"It's okay, buddy, one step at a time. Let me get the nurse."

Within moments the room swarmed with people. Everyone talked at once. The sounds reverberated through his head until he wanted to scream, *Stop!* He shut his eyes. A slight shake of his head, which sent spasms of anguish hurling through his entire body, silenced those around him. He sighed, swallowed hard and opened his eyes again.

"Water." The word whispered through his parched throat and sent an ache to the pit of his stomach. Someone heard. A straw pressed against his lips.

"Easy, now, just a few sips," a soft voice insisted, and an angelic face swam into view.

After the initial shock of cold liquid shivered through him, he drew another sip, and then another, as though he were dying of thirst, would be dead if not for her.

"Thank you," he rasped, then closed his eyes and drifted back to sleep. Some time later, the excited hum of voices penetrated his consciousness, and he awoke once more.

With extreme caution, he opened one eye enough to peek through his lashes, grateful to find most of the lights turned low. A relieved sigh shuddered through him, and the same unfamiliar face came into view.

"Hello again, buddy. How ya feeling?"

Rafe took a deep breath and exhaled on the knife-edge of pain. "Hurt. All over."

The shaggy head above him nodded. "Bet you do. Shall I call the nurse?"

Rafe shook his head, desperate for answers to the questions rattling around in his brain.

"I imagine you got a lot of questions; I'll try and answer them. You're in the hospital in Gillette, Wyoming. Been here close to two months now, in a coma the entire time. Got busted up pretty bad by that old bull, but doc said yesterday that everything is healed, physically anyway. No doubt you got a long road ahead of you with therapy and all. Anything I leave out?"

Rafe smiled at the disjointed English and chopped sentences of the dark-haired, olive-skinned man of obvious Hispanic descent. "Only one," he whispered, his throat ragged, voice raw. "Who are you?"

A huge belly laugh rumbled from deep within the barrel-sized chest. "Bud Jackson."

Rafe frowned while the name circled in his brain. "Do I know you? Should I?"

Bud grinned. "Not as well as I know you."

Rafe smiled in response to the chuckle in the old cowboy's voice and closed his eyes once more. "Remedy that," he mumbled and slid back into the peaceful realm of sleep.

The next morning Rafe awoke to the grumbling of his stomach. Careful of his broken body, he accepted Bud's help to sit upright and allowed the man to spoon-feed him the clear broth then flavored gelatin dietary sent up. Though very little actual sustenance, the fare filled the empty hole in his belly and revived his spirits.

"So how long have I been here?"

"Right near two months."

"What happened?"

"What do you remember?"

Rafe closed his eyes and tried to recall the incident that landed him flat on his back in a hospital. Sensations more than memories assailed him, gut-wrenching fear, rippling pain, total darkness. "Bull ride went all wrong. Don't recall how or why though."

Bud pointed his thumb upward. "Someone up there must be looking after you, you're lucky to be alive."

A knock on the door interrupted before either could delve deeper into the subject and the doctor walked in. "Well, I'll be. Had no way of knowing when or if you'd ever decide to wake up but look at you now! How do you feel today, Mr. Judson?"

A frown preceded his words. "Rough, Doc. Just sitting up for the last few minutes has me aching all over. How long will I be like this? What's the next step?" The doctor held up a hand to ward off the deluge of questions.

"First we need to run a few tests to determine if there's been any damage to your brain. All of your bones have healed and full recovery from those injuries will take a few weeks. You've been out for nearly two months, allow yourself at least that long to get back on your feet."

"But I don't have that long. I need to be back on the circuit so I can pay the bills I'm sure are piling up."

"You don't worry about that, none," Bud interrupted. "Concentrate on getting well."

"He's right," the doctor added. "Concentrate on getting well and figuring what you're going to do with the rest of your life. We had to put your hip and leg back together with plates and screws, so bull riding is out of the question."

"Rodeo is all I know."

"I'm sure that's not true, but if so, then I'd suggest you spend some time in prayer and see what it is God has in store for you next."

Rafe snorted. "Last I remember God and I weren't on good speaking terms."

The doctor patted his knee. "Never too late to change that," he said before he exited the room. Moments later a nurse came in and prepared to take Rafe down to radiology for tests.

Hours later he returned to the room, exhausted and in pain. Although he hated the pills, he readily accepted the offer of relief from the ache that consumed his entire body. Once again, Bud spoon-fed him the soft, bland foods on his tray, but Rafe insisted on drinking the beverages without assistance.

After lunch he settled down for a long nap and awoke in the early evening to find Bud snoring in the lounge chair next to the bed. He sat for long moments and wondered about the man who, from what he could tell, had become his constant companion. His mind circled on what the doctor said about the extent of his injuries and what he'd do with the rest of his life.

Pray.

The directive shocked him, shook his confidence to the core. Pray for what? Hope? Healing? Direction? What good is prayer to a broken up cowboy, especially one who had no room in his life for a God who didn't care?

Before he could contemplate the answers to the questions plaguing his mind, the doctor walked in, and Bud woke up.

The man thumbed through the chart alternately humming and grunting over the reports. "Good news and bad."

"Give me the bad first."

"The hip is not healing as fast as we thought. There are still weak areas around the plate we put in there to hold everything together. The good news is, there is no brain damage at all and with a few weeks of continued rest then therapy, you should be able to walk again, albeit with a limp."

Rafe closed his eyes on a moan. "So, rodeo is definitely out like you said."

"Yep, but there are plenty of jobs for a cowboy around here. You may be able to ride again, some day. Won't be easy and, chances are always painful, but possible. I'm sure other opportunities will come your way."

"What about the bills? I have some insurance, but I'm sure I've gone well beyond the total benefits available."

"Not the least bit worried," the doctor assured. "I'm sure you can make arrangements to pay after you get out of here. Besides, we have programs for those who can't pay. I'll see to it that a social worker comes up tomorrow and we'll start getting those things ironed out. As I said earlier, you just concentrate on getting back on your feet."

Rafe thanked him and turned to Bud after the doctor left. "So, what do you suggest?"

Bud grinned and offered only one solution. "Pray."

Rafe frowned.

"You got a problem with talking to God?"

Rafe heaved a sigh and closed his eyes. "I've had a problem with God since my mother died ten years ago."

"Goes deeper than that for you to stay mad at Him for ten years."

Rafe's throat constricted. He swallowed hard but refrained from comment. Bud's comment was right on target. His mind wandered back over the years, before the death of his mother, to his earliest memory and the horror inflicted on him in the name of God.

Constant shunning from his peers. Harsh treatment from staff at the "Christian" school he attended. The condemnation he felt and eternal damnation he expected due to his illegitimacy, despite his mother's assurance otherwise. Tears pricked his eyes, burned the back of his throat. Something had to show in his face for he felt a tender hand on his arm.

"Want to talk about it?"

Bud's soft voice reflected his concern. Rafe shook his head. He couldn't talk about it. Not now. Not ever.

"Must be pretty bad for you to keep bottled up inside for so long, but let me tell you from experience, buddy, bitterness and unforgiveness will destroy the best of men. You're listening to one of them. Cost me everything. You rest now. I'm gonna go out for a bite of supper. Want me to bring you something?"

Rafe's mouth watered at the thought of some real food. He smiled. "I'd give my right arm for a hamburger, fries and chocolate malt."

Bud chuckled. "You da man."

His laughter echoed in the room long after Bud left and eased the sting of memories assailing Rafe's heart and mind. Bud returned a short while later and they ate in companionable silence.

Bud groaned and stretched his legs then lowered his hat over his brow as though to settle in for another night then shifted. "Think I'll sleep in my own bed tonight since you're up and at it."

"Of course, you should. Thank you for everything."

Bud nodded. "See you tomorrow."

Night settled down around him and Rafe dozed off. He awoke in a cold sweat, shuddering from dreams he couldn't remember, but with an eerie sense of fear and foreboding. He tried to shut out the feelings and rest, but every time he closed his eyes, his heart raced, and muscles tensed until he ached all over.

He reached up and pulled the switch to turn on the overhead light then adjusted the bed to an upright position. He considered calling the nurse to bring him something for the pain but decided against it for fear of the addictive side effects. With as much care as possible, he leaned over and rummaged through the drawer of the bedside table in search of reading material but only came up with a bible. The word *pray* rang in his ears and echoed in his spirit.

He closed his eyes, cleared his throat, and whispered, "Lord, I know we haven't always been on the best of terms but there's got to be a reason I'm still alive. I'd appreciate if You would give me a clue to why and some idea of what the future holds."

He opened the book and began to read..... *"For I know the plans I have for you," says the* LORD. *"They are plans for good and not for disaster, to give you a future and a hope..."*

Hours later he closed the book, lowered the bed, turned off the light and fell into a restful sleep.

The next morning, he awoke, hungry as a bear and impatient to get out of bed. A social worker came in and advised him of the status of his insurance benefits and other options. Bud arrived shortly after breakfast, and they discussed what the lady told him. Later they wheeled him down for the first in a long string of painful days and restless nights while undergoing physical therapy.

Chapter Five

Rafe Judson made his way to the arena with a smile on his lips, a song in his heart, and the same old limp in his stride. An ex-bull-rider, he still loved everything about the rodeo...the scents—the hay, the horseflesh, the sweat—the excitement, the crowds. As a minister, he didn't enjoy the accidents or the deaths. He could do without a lot of the language, too.

Remember where you came from old boy.

The thought brought with it a quick stab of conviction.

I remember, Lord.

Wasn't so long ago he'd cussed and caroused along with the other cowboys. But all that changed with the accident that ended his career as a champion rodeo rider, but opened a whole new world to him, a world filled with faith and optimism.

Far cry from the cynical, bitter cowboy he once was.

Rafe always thought bull riding was his calling. Now he knew better. He'd found his true calling as prayer partner to hundreds of rodeo riders who passed through the area and as associate pastor of Cowboy Up Church in Recluse, Wyoming. The same town that nearly took his life three years ago now owned his heart as no other place had.

The influx of rodeo riders, regular and new, kept him busy on Saturday and filled the pews on Sunday. For both, he was grateful. He arrived at the arena, made his way up to the announcers' box and took his seat.

"Hey Rafe, how's it going?" Emcee, Bud Jackson asked.

"Great, Bud. You?"

"Just fine. There's a party at the Wild Horse Saloon tonight, gonna see you there?" Bud replied and snickered along with the others in the box.

"Gonna see you in church tomorrow?"

"Only if you promise to turn water into wine," Bud answered to the delight of the crew of announcers, judges, and clock watchers.

Rafe laughed at the familiar joke, took the ribbing in stride, and waited for his turn at the microphone. Bud Jackson was not only a faithful attendee at Cowboy Up, but one of Rafe's greatest supporters and friends. The opening prayer followed the Pledge of Allegiance and the Star Spangled Banner.

Rafe asked God's blessings on the event and for the safety of the cowboys and girls, the fans, and especially the clowns who many times risked their life to save a cowboy. He asked special favor on the emergency medical technicians who also often faced danger in their attempt to get an injured cowboy or girl out of the arena. He then made his way out of the box and down to the bull pens, holding pens, and paddocks to chat and pray with those who wanted to.

A flash of movement out of the corner of his eye caught his attention. He turned to watch a young woman attempt to mount her horse. The animal snorted, stomped his foot, and swerved away from her. She fell to the ground with a thud. His eyebrows shot up in surprise at the muttered curse which fell from her lips before she burst into tears. He hurried over to where she sat in the mud and manure.

"Are you hurt?"

She shook her head. "No. Stupid horse."

Rafe reached to help her up. She staggered against him. He turned his face away from the pungent odor of alcohol mixed with horse manure. "Let's get you out of here. Are you sure you're not hurt?"

She shook her head, wobbled on her feet. "No, just help me up on my horse."

"You're in no shape to ride. What's your name?"

"Just who do you think you are to tell me I can't ride? Just 'cause you're a preacher or something don't mean you can tell me what I can and can't do."

Rafe wrapped an arm around her waist and hauled her against him. "Well, I'm not going to help you onto that horse even if he would stand still for you to mount, which I bet he won't. And that means he has more sense than you if you try."

She leaned into him, almost tumbled them both, and took a deep breath. "You smell good, preacher man. What's that cologne?"

He chuckled. "None, but I'm sure your senses are so filled with booze and horse manure anything smells better."

She stared up at him, wide-eyed. "You mean you smell this good on your own? Must be the soap you use then, 'cause no cowboy smells this good. And believe me, I've smelled plenty. No preacher I ever met does either. What's your name preacher man?"

"Rafe Judson. What's yours?"

"Lori Strickland."

"Where are you from, Lori?"

"Bandera, Texas."

"Nice town. How old are you?"

"Twenty-five. How old are you?"

Rafe eased her down on a bale of hay and sat beside her. "Thirty."

"Wow, young to be crippled. What happened?"

"Got hung up on a bull three years ago and almost lost my life. I'm lucky to be here at all, much less be able to walk, even with a limp."

No surprise when her eyes widened another notch.

"You're a bull rider?"

He nodded. "Was."

She snuggled closer, nuzzled the skin beneath his ear and whispered, "I love bull riders."

Rafe ignored the shivers incited by her sensuous deed and moved her out of his embrace. She puckered her lips into a sexy pout and hummed a suggestive purr. Though he tried to ward off her advance, she slid her arms around his neck and pressed herself against him in an intimate gesture, then passed out.

He glanced down at the young beauty in his arms with her cherub face, pixie mouth, and long, spiky lashes. *Now what?* Before he could consider what to do about her, a low-keyed wolf-whistle assaulted his ears.

"Well, if that don't beat all I've ever seen, preacher man with a woman in his arms. In public no less."

Rafe glared up at his long-time rival Jedediah Johnson. "It's not what you think."

Jed snorted. "Sure it ain't."

"Get your mind out of the gutter, Jed and help me figure out what to do with her. I don't know if she's got a room or not. Her horse is over there." He nodded at the stout sorrel gelding across the way. "I have no idea if she's alone or with someone, or even where her trailer is parked."

Jed's ribald laughter crawled up his spine and made every hair on the back of Rafe's neck stand at attention.

"I know what I'd do with a pretty little filly like that, drunk or not." His eyes raked over her, lips curled. "Unless I'm mistaken, I already have."

Torn between the need to protect her and an unholy desire to break Jed's jaw, Rafe rose with her in his arms. "That's exactly why I can't leave her here, alone, for the likes of you to take advantage of." He turned on his heel and stalked off as much as his bum leg would allow.

Sorry excuse for a man. And he calls himself a cowboy. Don't understand why he can't get over the past, it's not like I'm competing anymore.

He and Jed had been rivals forever, always tried to outdo one another. But that was over, in the past and, much as he tried to show grace and mercy, he just couldn't tolerate Jed's cavalier attitude. Chances are by morning the whole town would know he'd been caught with a woman. Jed's convoluted version of the story of course.

Rafe sighed. *Oh well, Lord, You know the truth and that's all that matters.*

Lori moaned and twisted in his arms. Rafe felt her muscles convulse, heard the telltale gurgle in her throat, and turned her over moments before she vomited all over his shirt. His boots weren't so lucky.

His stomach lurched in response, but he managed to swallow the bile that pooled in his throat. By some stroke of fate or a miracle, he made it to his truck. He propped his foot up on the side-step, held her draped across one leg and shoulder, and fumbled in his pocket for the keys. He opened the door and poured her inside.

With no alternative he could think of, he drove to his cabin and laid her in his bed. By the time he finished, he struggled for the slightest breath and his hip and leg ached. Still, his night wasn't over, so he locked the door behind him, hitched up his old horse trailer and drove back to the rodeo until the event ended. He fetched her horse and loaded him in the trailer then took him home too. He'd know tomorrow which vehicle and trailer was hers. Until then, he'd do what he had to do.

He'd sleep on the couch.

Chapter Six

Lori awoke to the aroma of bacon, eggs, and coffee. Her stomach seized and clutched like a nervous fist. Her head pounded in rhythm to the footsteps in the other room. Her eyes were mere slits but even the tiny amount of light allowed, glared like a car beam in the dead of night. She whimpered and rolled onto her side. Thoughts revolved in cadence with the painful throb in her head and heaving of her stomach. *Where am I? How did I get here?*

She passed her hand along the fabric of her shirt and jeans then wriggled her toes. Relief poured through her when she realized the only thing missing was her boots. Unlike some of the other times she woke up in a strange bed. The footsteps came closer, hesitated, then moved across the room to close the blinds. *Blessed relief.*

His scent preceded him...musky, spicy, male and she remembered the preacher. *Oh, no, what have I done?*

She opened her eyes again. Her vision swam then focused on him. She pushed herself into an upright position. The motion caused everything to sway and lurch. A trashcan materialized. She hung her head and retched until she figured she had no stomach left. She felt his weight on the bed beside her and a cool, damp cloth brush over her face. She sighed.

"Thank you. I think."

He chuckled and the sound reverberated in her head. She moaned and pressed the heels of her hands against her eyes. He whispered an apology then asked if she'd like coffee or aspirin. She nodded and somehow managed to get the words *please* and *black* through her raw throat.

The items appeared before her within minutes. Her hand trembled when she took the cup. She reached for the aspirin then swallowed them with one sip of the hot brew. The caffeine shot straight through her system and, in less time than she took to finish the mug of java, the headache disappeared.

"Think you're up to a bite of breakfast, or would you prefer dry toast?"

"Toast is fine."

"Would you like to take a shower? I'll loan you a pair of sweats and a t-shirt and we can toss your clothes in the washer. I need to get over to the church but after service I'll take you and your horse to the campgrounds to fetch your vehicle and trailer."

She dared a look into the crystal blue eyes, surprised at the lack of judgment or condemnation there. A flush heated her cheeks. "Thanks."

Rafe brushed the hair off her face. "You're welcome. I'd invite you to church but doubt you'd be comfortable there in my clothes."

Humiliation warmed her face, her eyes narrowed. "Wouldn't want to embarrass you, either now would we preacher man?"

"Name's Rafe and let's get one thing straight. You wouldn't embarrass me. I could care less what people think, or say, as long as God and I know the truth. So, if you want to come to church, you're more than welcome. I just didn't want you to feel obligated to do so, compelled to make excuses why you couldn't, or ashamed if you preferred not to. Now, the bathroom's through there."

He nodded to an adjoining room then rose and walked to his dresser and pulled out the sweats and t-shirt and carried them back to her. "There's an extra toothbrush in the medicine cabinet. Just toss your clothes out the door and I'll throw them in the washer. If you need anything else, just holler."

She waited until he exited the room and stood on legs that wobbled. Even with his outburst, she'd seen compassion in his steadfast gaze. She clutched the clothes to her chest and made her way with great care into the bathroom. One look in the mirror above the sink and she burst into tears. She may not have seen condemnation or judgment in his eyes, but she couldn't escape what reflected in hers.

She hurried and turned on the water so he wouldn't hear her pitiful sobs then stripped off her clothes, opened the door a notch, and deposited them in a heap on the floor. She eased the shower curtain back and stepped under the hot, steamy stream then collapsed under the weight of guilt and condemnation in her heart.

Oh God, how have I fallen so far?

Lori never considered herself religious or devout. Not since the day she decided to embark on a rodeo career had she remotely felt God's presence or heard His voice. But never in her wildest dreams did she imagine her life as it reflected back to her in the mirror moments ago. Dark circles enhanced the ghastly gray pallor of her skin. Her blood-shot eyes were swollen and puffy. The scent of alcohol oozed from her very pores. Her stomach churned. Saliva pooled in her mouth. She swallowed hard.

Visions of her life over the last few years rose in her mind, filling the shower with a foul stench. What would her parents think if they knew how far she'd slid down the slippery slope of sin? What would Stanley or Amber think?

Her stomach revolted as the questions rolled around in her brain. Bile rose in her throat. She slapped the water nozzle aside so as not to flood the floor then jerked the curtain aside, stretched across the tub, and hung her head over the commode until nothing but dry heaves shuddered through her.

Dragging herself to her feet, she stood on wobbly legs and weakened knees to embrace the warm water. The clean scent of anti-bacterial soap helped cleanse the grit and grime of her night, but she doubted anything could wash away the shame in her heart.

* * *

Rafe waited until he heard the water start to run before he went into the bedroom and picked up her clothes. The sound of her sobs twisted his heart and he reached for the doorknob then hesitated.

Can't just walk in there like you would have three years ago, old boy. Not proper.

He ground his teeth at the gentle admonishment and forced himself to move away from the door and over to the bed to pull the quilted cover off his mattress. The short trip to the laundry room did little to ease the turmoil in his mind. Sometimes the restrictions put on him by his calling chafed to the core. A low growl sounded in his throat when he tossed the items into the washer and added a liberal dose of detergent but didn't turn the machine on until he heard the water stop running in the bathroom.

Rafe returned to the kitchen, popped two pieces of bread into the toaster, and placed a saucer and fresh cup of coffee on the table then added butter, jelly and peanut butter as Lori walked into the room. His heart tripped over itself at the anguish in her chocolate eyes and he fought the urge to take her in his arms. She sat in the chair he'd pulled away from the table, unfolded the napkin across her lap and looked up at him. Her lip trembled, eyes filled.

She looked like a lost angel—sad, forlorn.

"I'm sorry for being such a b..." She bit off the word, flushed. "Witch."

He chuckled and placed the bread on her saucer. "Your original choice of words would be a little more apt to describe your behavior but thank you for not saying it. And you are most certainly forgiven."

She smiled and his heart skipped a thud. She bit into the dry toast, and he could tell she tested her stomach to see if it would accept the meager fare before she took another bite.

"You're not like any other preacher I've met," she observed.

"What are the other preachers like?"

"Rude, arrogant, snobbish, not one I know would have talked with me drunk as I was, much less brought me to their house and put me in their bed."

Rafe knew she spoke the truth. Still, he held himself in no regard above others. He shrugged. "Didn't see any other solution. Had no idea which trailer was yours, or how I'd get you into it. Certainly, didn't want to dig through your pockets for keys and I knew there were no rooms available within a fifty mile radius."

He smiled and ran his hand over her hair in a gentle caress. "So here we are."

A shiver vibrated through him at the contact and reminded him of when he was not a preacher, but a mere man. That one, simple touch sparked a truth to light in his mind: *Even an earnest or innocent gesture can easily turn into something less than honorable.*

She glanced up at him, her eyes alive with emotions. Heat climbed up his neck and infused his face. He averted his gaze and groped for a response to the blatant invitation in hers.

"Guess I've been a cowboy much longer than a preacher and no respectable cowboy would leave a woman in distress, even the self-inflicted kind." He glanced at his watch.

"I need to get over to the church. Just make yourself comfortable and when I return, I'll drive you to the campgrounds."

Her soft voice halted his escape. "Rafe, I think you're a wonderful cowboy and I bet an even better preacher."

He shook his head with a rueful smile. "I've got a long way to go to be even a good preacher, but thanks."

***

Lori finished her toast and coffee then cleaned the dishes. Afterward, she put the laundry on to dry and scrubbed the bathroom. Although one could tell the structure was solely male dominated, she liked the tidy little house and found pleasure in picking up after him. He filled every room the same way he crowded her mind.

To use the word handsome to describe the man would be an understatement, despite the limp in his stride. The mere thought of his crystal blue eyes sent shivers along every nerve in her body. His dark hair fell over his forehead in roughish waves and made her fingers itch to run through the silken strands to see if they were as soft as they appeared.

Well proportioned for his height, his broad chest and muscular arms made her want to curl up in his embrace. Long, slim, legs and muscled thighs were definite attributes that bespoke the label *cowboy*, with a capital C. And the way those jeans clung to his lean hips... she trembled and blushed at her wayward thoughts. Toward a preacher no less!

Surrounded by his scent she took a deep breath. The aroma invaded her from head to toe. Her heart skittered and danced its way into her stomach, did a slow swirl, then settled with a joyous little flip. Amused at herself, Lori shook her head. *He's certainly invaded my sphere.*

She wandered into the bedroom, searched out fresh sheets and remade the bed. She put the dirty linen along with the towel and facecloth she used into the machine to wash then walked around and admired his collection of trophies and ribbons. Funny she'd never heard of him since his rodeo success was one of record-breaking sensation.

Photos and newspaper articles recounted his entire career up to the time of his accident. Her heart ached when she read how he got hung up on a bull and then stomped when the animal shook him loose. He'd suffered broken ribs, a shattered leg, and a busted pelvis and lain in a coma for weeks. The fact he lived, much less walked, was indeed a miracle.

The buzzer on the dryer sounded, so she changed into her clothes and spread the quilt over the clean sheets on his bed. She then tossed the other load into the machine to dry and turned it on. She tugged on her boots and walked out the back door to locate her horse. The minute she stepped outside, the odor of stale vomit assaulted her nostrils.

She looked down, saw his boots, and grimaced. Her stomach quivered but she ignored the queasiness, picked up the offensive objects, carried them over to the facet and turned on the water. She rinsed the mess off then went back inside to scrub and polish them to a high-gloss shine.

She glanced at her watch. *Ten-thirty*. If his church service was anything like what she and her family attended back in Bandera, he'd be there until noon. She had no idea what she'd do with herself for another hour-and-a-half. She opened the refrigerator and examined the contents to see if there was something she could prepare for lunch then canned that idea. If he was like the preacher back home, he'd have a dozen invitations to dine at someone's house after services.

She sighed and tore a slip of paper off the magnetic note pad attached to the refrigerator door, took the pen out of its holder, and, in a few short words, thanked him for his kindness and hospitality. On impulse she jotted her cell phone number on the bottom.

Not that I *expect* to hear from him, she thought, and laid the note on the table. She went out the back way, careful to lock the door behind her. Solomon grazed in a small corral. Her tack hung on a peg in the tiny lean-to. She saddled and bridled the horse and rode around the house, hesitated, and looked around. The campground was easy to spot across the clear horizon.

Though surrounded by mountains, not much marred the landscape surrounding the small Wyoming town slightly northwest of Gillett and Lori knew she'd have no trouble finding her way back to where her truck and trailer waited.

***

Rafe knew she'd left before he opened the door and found her note. His heart felt as empty as the house. Not much larger than a cabin or cottage, he always thought the home too small but now it felt huge. *Funny how one person could make such a difference.* He dared not dwell on the effect she had on him or how many ways she touched his heart. He dug out the ingredients for a sandwich and salad then prepared himself a bite to eat. After he ate, he cleaned up and tried to rest, but couldn't get her off his mind.

His physical reaction was feral, would be for any man. Her thick blonde hair invited one to sink his hands in the heavy mass and wallow in the luxurious weight and softness. He could drown in those chocolate colored eyes with their long, silky lashes. Her pert little nose and perfect bow-shaped mouth reminded him of a porcelain doll. Both begged to be kissed.

He took a deep breath and recalled her scent as she smelled this morning...fresh, clean, female. His heartbeat thickened to a slow thud, body tightened. His fists curled with want, mouth watered for a taste of her lips.

A groan escaped along with the breath lodged in his throat. He dry washed his face and raked both hands through his hair. Celibacy had never been his strong point, although through grace he hadn't actually battled with it until now. She had the face of an angel and a figure designed for pleasure for sure, but his attraction extended far beyond sheer animal magnetism, intensified in a way he'd yet to experience.

What is it about her, Lord?

He closed his eyes and envisioned her as she looked dressed in his clothes, all of which swallowed her small frame. She'd reminded him of a waif—lost, alone, afraid. The torment in her eyes went much deeper than shame over her behavior. *Soul deep.*

He recognized the emotions that had been so much a part of him not so long ago and the means by which he'd tried to banish them. Drugs, booze, and sex were all means of escape from the emptiness in a heart, the dark hunger of a soul. He had no doubt she dabbled in every vice.

His heart clenched at the thought of her offering that beautiful body to just anyone, for less than honorable reasons. Jed's suggestive comments last night echoed in his mind. His hands curled into fists and his stomach lurched when he realized he'd once been no better than his adversary in that respect.

Once upon a time, but no more.

The thought brought little comfort when he considered his physical reactions to her.

What if she ran into Jed or someone like him on the way back to the campgrounds? Fear stabbed his heart as vicious thoughts of *what if* assaulted his mind. He snapped the recliner into an upright position and vaulted from the chair in one fluid motion then tugged on his boots, slapped his hat on his head, and left the house.

He returned two hours later disheartened because she was nowhere to be found. He picked up the note she'd left, traced the number on the bottom of the page with his thumb.

Unease stirred his spirit as his mind replayed last night and the condition he found her in. And this morning...the soul deep pain in her eyes, the lure of temptation she possessed, the blatant invitation in her gaze....

He focused on the pain, ignored the rest. Just going to call to make sure she's safe, he told himself. Twin blades of relief and disappointment cut through him when the phone went straight to voicemail.

"Hey Lori, its Rafe. Just wanted to make sure you got back to the arena safe and sound. Let me know. If you want to, that is. Umm, okay, well, bye. Oh, and take care."

He rattled off his number then hung up feeling like a fool, pretty sure he sounded like one too. He hated talking to machines.

Chapter Seven

Lori sat in the middle of her bed and clutched an old teddy bear to her chest. After travelling the rodeo circuit nearly a year, it felt good to be back in Bandera. She hadn't been able to get Rafe Judson off her mind, not during the long miles between Wyoming and Texas, nor in the weeks that followed.

She'd listened to his message more than once. She'd tried a couple of times to return his call and left a message that she was fine on his voicemail but hadn't actually spoken to him. *Which was probably for the best.*

More than shame filled her heart when she thought about the way she'd acted toward him. Desire rode the heels of embarrassment trailed by humiliation whenever he came to mind. Not since her childhood crush on Stanley Morrison had she been this entranced with a man.

Her cell phone interrupted her thoughts. Lori glanced at the caller id then chatted with one of her high school friends, ending with a promise to get together soon. The reminiscing brought back memories of the time she'd tried to break up Stanley and Amber when she was fifteen. How she'd lied and whispered behind his back and how, despite all of that, both had forgiven her.

Even now, she remained friends with Stan's wife, and adored his children. Still, she envied the woman for capturing the heart of the most sincere man she'd ever met. Stanley was a true cowboy in every sense of the word—honest, loyal, chivalrous, *faithful*.

In the years since Stan and Amber wed, Lori searched high and low for another man like him only to be disappointed time and again, until Rafe, and she had no idea what to do. There was no doubt in her heart he'd be every bit the cowboy of her dreams but the fact he was a preacher scared the daylights out of her.

A preacher!

Who'd have ever thought Roy Strickland's 'wild child' would tumble boots over spurs for a preacher?

A knock on the door pulled her thoughts from their wanderings. Her father entered at her bidding.

"What's up, Princess?"

"Just thinking."

"About...?"

She eyed him for a long, thoughtful moment. Teenage rebellion had caused her to shun her father's efforts to be close. Not too much of course, after all, she knew where her bread was buttered, and she knew how to play him to get what she wanted, had learned that trait from early childhood. A pang of remorse stabbed her heart and she smiled and moved over so he could sit beside her on the bed.

"I met a man, Daddy, a wonderful man and he's got me twisted up in knots."

"Not again," he grumbled his voice something between a groan and a chuckle and reached out to brush her hair off her shoulders. "Who is it this time?"

Lori's cheeks stung at her father's banter, but she couldn't blame him for feeling that way after the parade of men and boys she'd brought home over the years. "His name is Rafe Judson and he's a cowboy preacher."

Surprise registered on his face. "Rafe Judson, *the* Rafe Judson, bull-rider extraordinaire?"

She nodded.

"He's a preacher you said?"

"Yeah, took up the calling after his accident three years ago."

"Wow. Where'd you meet him?"

"At the rodeo in Recluse, Wyoming."

"Well, what about him has you tied up in knots?"

She rolled her eyes, flung herself backward, and clutched the teddy bear tighter. "He's a preacher!"

This time her father did chuckle. "Could be worse, could be a bum like the last guy you brought home." He dug his fingers into her ribs and made her laugh.

"Yeah, but can you imagine me with a preacher? There's no way on earth people would accept me as a preacher's wife."

He eyed her, concern and curiosity lit his midnight gaze. "What makes you say that?"

Her cheeks heated, eyes lowered. Mortification laced her tone. "Oh, Daddy, I'm not a princess and nowhere near a saint. If you knew half the things I've done you'd disown me."

His eyes took on a tender glow. He pulled her in his arms and stroked her hair as he had when she was little and hadn't in a long time. His voice deepened with conviction.

"Every little girl is born to be a princess. God designed it that way. And you listen to me Lori Beth, I don't care what you've done I'll always love you. I may be disappointed, hurt or even angry but you are my child. Flesh of my flesh and heart of my heart and nothing will ever change that." He shifted her in his embrace and smiled into her eyes.

"Never forget the story of the prodigal son. Besides, sometimes the lower a person falls, the stronger the conviction, deeper the redemption, and greater the testimony. If you have feelings for this man, you owe it to yourself and him to be honest about it. Time will tell if what you feel is more than infatuation."

That he used her full name told her how serious her father was. He never called her by her given name, always Honey or Pumpkin or Princess. In fact, the only time he called her *Lori Beth* was when he wanted to make a strong point, or when she was in trouble.

Lori smiled and hugged his neck for the first time in a long time with true devotion. "Thanks, Daddy."

If he believed in her so much, maybe Rafe would too. *If only she could be good enough.*

Her father clung to her a moment and continued to stroke her long, blonde locks then kissed her cheek. "You're welcome, Princess," he said then left her alone once more.

Lori cuddled the bear again and allowed the dream of being Mrs. Rafe Judson to fill her with excitement and hope. She had no idea how she'd manage to change her ways to that of a preacher's wife or even where to start. She'd always been wild and rebellious despite her family's attempts to instill Christian virtues into her heart and mind.

A sense of panic enveloped her. Could she ever be good enough to win the heart much less the hand of a preacher? Could she ever be good enough for God?

Forget it Lori, you'll never be good enough. Besides, good girls have no fun.

Uncomfortable now, she tossed the bear aside, swung out of bed and into her boots then went to practice on the barrels.

The good thing about riding the circuit is there's no time to think of anything but the next rodeo.

* * *

Lori urged Solomon into a full gallop around the barrels then brought him to a sliding stop along the fence beside Stanley. "How'd we do?" She'd barely been home two days when he showed up to continue Solomon's training.

Stan glanced at the stopwatch and smiled. "Doing great, Lors, shaved two minutes off your time since our last training session. You should be getting close to Pro status now. How'd the last rodeo go, where was it again?"

Heat singed her neck and face. She slid from the saddle, and avoided his gaze, unable to tell him she'd forfeited her last rodeo. "Recluse, Wyoming, not so well."

She tugged on the cinch and loosened her saddle.

"Both you and Solomon are doing great. I've no doubt you'll do better next time and catch up. When do you head out again?"

She flushed at the compliment, more ashamed now at how low she'd sunk considering his hard work and confidence in her. "Thanks Stanley, you know how much I value your opinion. Not sure when I'm heading out, thought I'd take a short break from it all."

Stanley fell in step beside her when she started walking Solomon to cool him down.

"Is something wrong, Lors? You don't seem happy despite your success."

She shrugged. "Just tired, I guess. And disappointed."

"Well then it's a good thing you're taking a break. There's no sense in pushing yourself or your horse. If you're tired, it's a sure bet he is. I know your parents are glad you'll be home a while. I know they've missed you. We all have. We support you, but it's worrisome to have you out there alone and gone for so long."

Lori's heart cringed. *If only they knew.* She headed toward the barn and unsaddled Solomon while Stanley removed the horse's bridle and put a halter on him. Lori grabbed the grooming supplies and met him at the washing station where he hosed Solomon down. She tossed him a brush.

"I understand everyone's concern over me riding the circuit, and I appreciate it. I really do, but I can take care of myself."

Yeah, right, like you did in Wyoming.

Lori ground her teeth and ignored the sneering voice in her head. "Daddy still thinks I ought to go to college, but what good is that when I have no idea what I want to do? Even if I could stand the thought of going back, I don't know what I want to be when I grow up." A humorless laugh escaped her.

"You'd think at nearly twenty-six, I would have some idea, but I'm clueless. One thing I do know is that I want bigger and better than what I can find in this dinky little town. Surely you understand that. Look where you came from and what you've built, the name and reputation you've carved for yourself. And you've had no formal education."

Stanley shook his head and sighed. He turned off the water, rolled the hose on its rack, untied Solomon and led him into his stall while Lori put away the grooming supplies. They met at the barn door and continued their conversation.

"Sometimes all you need is talent combined with common sense and a healthy dose of faith, but Lori, carving a name for yourself takes time and commitment. I never understood your feelings about Bandera. It's beautiful here and you won't find more community-minded people anywhere.

"But I guess some of us have to leave the place we've known all our life, spread our wings and find greener pastures. But remember one thing Lors, the grass is usually greener over the septic tank. Fame and fortune doesn't always equal happiness. True happiness comes from within."

She took a step nearer, rested her head against his chest. "Then why is happiness so hard for me?" Her voice quivered. She swallowed the hard knot of tears in her throat.

Stanley ran his hands over her shoulders and back in a soothing gesture then stepped back. "It's like looking for love in all the wrong places. If you're expecting someone or some *thing* to make you happy, it'll never happen. Oh, you might be joyous with the next victory or the right boyfriend, but true happiness is inside you. What do you think it'll take to make you truly happy? What are you most passionate about?"

He shook his head to ward off her words. "I don't need the answer Lori, but you have to figure that out. Really, deep down consider. Write it down if you have to. Then every morning think and pray on that dream, do what you can to work toward it, then let go and let God bring it to pass in His time."

"You make it sound so easy, but I've wanted the same thing for years and have yet to get it."

"Mind if I ask what 'it' is?"

Lori took a deep breath, hesitated, and then took a chance on confiding in her best friend, someone she knew wouldn't laugh or make her feel simple and small. "I want a husband and family. A cowboy. Someone like you. A man who loves and adores me and whom I can love and adore back. *That's* what I'm passionate about."

"Well, then, maybe what you *think* will make you happy is not what God knows you need. Have you asked Him?"

"No, not really," Lori admitted. "I don't know how. I mean, I believe in God but I'm not sure I buy into all the hoopla. Think about it, one day we're admonished to forgive and forget, and the next made to believe God is some vengeful Being who watches our every move, ready to send us to hell in a moments notice.

"Then, we're told about this father-like figure full of love and grace and mercy. Which is true? On top of all that, there's all these rules and regulations.... don't do this, shouldn't do that. I feel like I can't even breathe without the chance of being punished, much less have a life with any degree of fun."

Stanley shook his head. "That's exactly where you're mistaken. God is so much more than anything you've heard or imagined and above all, He wants a personal, intimate relationship with you. Have you ever read the bible for yourself?"

She shook her head.

"Then that's what's missing in your life, and in your quest for the perfect man. There is no such thing. A man is not going to save you from anything--not this small town, not from boredom, not even from yourself. You need a savior for that. I know you've been baptized and all, but have you ever *truly* given your heart to God?"

Lori shrugged. "Just when I was *supposed* to. In Church."

"Then get alone with God. Spend some quiet, quality time in prayer and seek Him. Find your own truth about who He is. All you need is a bible, a willing heart, and an open mind to discover His true character and His purpose for your life. Forget everything you've heard or thought, forget about what Lori thinks she wants or needs, and focus on Him.

"If He wants you to have a husband, cowboy or otherwise, let Him bring that person to you. Bury yourself so deeply in His heart that your mate has to go through Him to find you. You have to be a whole person before you can be half a couple Lori, and God is the only one who can make you whole."

Before she could comment, a vehicle approached the barn. A frown crossed Stanley's face. "That's Amber," he remarked and strode toward the oncoming SUV.

Lori followed. Amber leaned out the window and caressed her husband's cheek.

"Hey, Lori, good to see you, congratulations on your winnings. Stanley's told me how hard you work. Looks like its still paying off."

"Thanks," Lori replied.

Stanley grinned. "That's cause she's got the best horse, born, bred, raised *and* trained by the best horseman in the state of Texas."

Amber rolled her eyes and turned to her sister-in-law, Lexie who sat in the passenger seat. "He's so modest."

Lexie grunted and leaned over to where she could see Lori better. "Whatever you do, don't marry a cowboy, especially a successful one. Their ego is impossible to sustain. Marry a doctor like Scott."

"Like there's no arrogance or conceit there," Amber muttered.

Stanley winked at Lori then turned back to address his wife and sister-in-law. "No arrogance or conceit here, either, just stating the facts, Ma'am."

Lori laughed at the exchange. "Like you two aren't ga ga over your cowboys."

Amber smiled at Stanley, caressed his cheek again and sighed. "Guilty. I just wanted to stop by and let you know we're headed into San Antonio. Ace and Daddy have all the kids. Want to come along, Lori?"

Lori's eyes widened. "Yeah, I'd love to. Can you give me a few minutes to freshen up?"

"Sure, take all the time you need."

"She seems troubled," Amber remarked as Lori hurried toward the house.

Stan nodded. "Having an identity crises."

"She reminds me of my friend Christy back in high school," Lexie stated. "Poor, little rich girl, has everything a body could ever want and yet, never satisfied. She committed suicide our junior year."

Stanley eyed her. "Then maybe you're the one to help her."

Lexie shook her head. "Couldn't help Christy, so I doubt I could do Lori any good. Besides, why would she listen to me? I'm the new kid in town, she barely knows me."

"Sometimes it's easier to talk to a stranger. Think about it," Stanley urged as Lori hurried toward them. She thanked him again, and then climbed into the SUV.

Stan leaned in for a kiss from his wife. "Okay. You three be careful and don't spend it all in one place."

"We won't," they chorused as Amber turned the vehicle around and they headed to town.

Chapter Eight

Lori dressed for her morning run. She'd been home a little over a month and already felt the repressive atmosphere of small town existence close in on her as it always had. The wanderlust that plagued her soul as long as she could remember rose up to choke her.

Embarrassment and humiliation rode the heels of shame when she thought about last night and how she'd fallen, again, despite her resolve not to. Since she arrived home and her subsequent chat with Stanley, she did her best to change her wild and wanton ways.

She stayed out of the bars and attended church with her family. She'd tried reading the bible but was more confused than before and 'quiet,' 'quality,' time alone with God didn't seem to work. Whenever she tried all she felt or recalled were sins and inadequacies.

Then last night the phone calls wouldn't stop. Old friends whom she avoided for weeks wouldn't take no for an answer.

"We'll just bar hop. Won't stay long in one place at all, might even drive into San Antonio."

"C'mon, there's nothing wrong with a couple of dances."

"You don't have to do anything you don't want to, just have a little fun."

And then there was the cowboy. The town *Romeo, Bandera's Stud, Cowboy Casanova,* he'd been called these and then some. She'd seen him before, been with him before. He had the looks—tall and handsome, the charm—suave and debonair, sweet talk, and smooth moves. Her body quivered even as her heart cringed. A flush heated her cheeks.

She picked up her pace as the sun peeked over the hills in a glorious display of light and color. These few moments when the morning was fresh, bright with promise and full of hope, nothing seemed impossible.

Nothing except changing your ways.

She heard the words deep in her spirit. A quick stab of guilt pierced her conscience. Her breath caught on a sob. She stopped, shook her head, and raised her eyes heavenward. "No, I guess that's not possible here. But where? How?"

Seek and ye shall find. Ask and ye shall receive. Knock and the door will be opened.

"I tried," she yelled at the heavens then fell to her knees on the hard, rocky earth. "It didn't work," she muttered and burst into tears.

"I'm s-sorry," she said between sobs. "B-but I don't know how to reach You."

A ray of sunshine glinted off an object and caught the corner of her eye. Lori turned and gazed out over the arena. A thought sparked: *time to move on again.*

Stanley's voice rose in her mind. "If you think riding the rodeo circuit is the answer, I'm afraid you'll be sadly mistaken."

He'd chastised her more than once that she was looking for love in all the wrong places.

"Oh, shut up will you," she mumbled and jogged back to the house. That evening she got online, checked schedules, and paid her entry fees for weeks in advance. Her heart stuttered when she noted the date for the next rodeo in Recluse, Wyoming.

That means I have six months to get my act together, she thought with renewed resolve, though she had no idea how she'd accomplish such a feat.

* * *

Flush with victory, Lori rode the shoulders of one cowboy while the beer flowed freely all around. He assisted as she slid down his back and twirled her in his arms for a two-step. She indulged him and a half-dozen other cowboys in a dance or two then slipped away, just as she had over the past couple of months. She hadn't overindulged on alcohol or woke up in some cowboy's bed since that last night in Bandera. She couldn't say she was happier with this new way of life, but at least she wasn't ashamed or guilty. The next morning, she bade his entrance when Maverick, a bronc buster and bull rider banged on the door of her living quarters.

"Hey, Lors, what'cha doin?"

She shot him a narrow eyed glance. "Don't call me Lors. No one except Stanley calls me that."

"Well ex-cu-se me. Who is Stanley? The source of your undying love?"

Lori rolled her eyes. She knew he teased but his tone grated. "Let's just say he's someone whose boots you're not fit to lick."

He swallowed a laugh, gave her a look of pained devastation, and covered his heart with his hat. "You cut deep, Lori."

She grinned. "Back at you, Maverick. Is there a purpose to this visit?"

His tone changed to one of genuine interest. "Just wondering what you're up to. You seem a little distant lately. What happened to my party girl?"

Lori sighed. "Don't you ever get tired of it all, Maverick, the constant partying and travelling with no substance or purpose, no real purpose, to your life?"

"What else is there?"

She fingered the Bible on her lap and shrugged. "Guess that's what I'm trying to find out."

He stepped closer, peered at the book she held then snorted. "Good luck with that, it never helped me much. Too many rules and regulations, nothing but backbiting and gossip. I mean, have you ever met anyone who really walks the walk? Most Christians" ... he finger-quoted the word for emphasis... "just as soon cuss you as bless you. Hell, if I can't drink a beer or two and dance with a pretty girl to celebrate getting off a bull or bucking bronc alive and in one piece, then I don't need it.

"Now, granted, mine is a small and narrow world but from what I see of the Church" ...again he finger-quoted the word.... "I'm better off dealing with my Maker when I meet Him or when I'm too old to ride anything but a rocking chair. But one thing's for certain, sweetheart, if you're gonna be good, be good. But if you're gonna be bad, might as well be all the way bad. There ain't no in-between. Not with them folks."

Before she could respond he pulled her in his arms and covered her lips in a kiss meant to stir the blood, released her, and then left.

Lori slumped into her chair, shaken to the core by his words and actions. *I guess he's right,* she thought. Other than her parents, Stanley, Amber, and their extended family, no one she could name actually acted on what they said they believed. In fact, most were as messed up as she.

Maverick's words rolled around in her head. *"If you're gonna be bad, might as well be all the way bad."*

"I don't know how to be any other way," she muttered. "And being good doesn't seem to make any difference."

Tears stung her eyes and clogged her throat. She pulled the Bible against her breast and rocked back and forth in her chair as the tiny flame of hope she'd carried around for weeks died.

She wept.

Her cell phone rang. Lori picked it up with the intention of sending the call straight to voicemail. Lexie Harris's name flashed on the screen. Fear seized her heart.

"Lexie, is something wrong?"

Lori's breath caught when Lexie hesitated in answering.

"Not here but I was about to ask you the same question. You sound upset, is something wrong?"

Lori ground her teeth to hold back a sob. "Umm, I'm just having a rough day. You scared me. I thought something was wrong with Stanley or Amber or one of the kids."

"I didn't mean to frighten you. I hope you don't mind Stanley giving me your number. It's just that, you've been on my heart and mind for a while now and I felt the Lord urge me to call and check on you."

Lori doubted that but thanked her anyway and assured Lexie she was fine.

Chapter Nine

Rafe Judson sent the chair on his porch rocking with one push of his boot against the floor. On his thigh rested a bible, Lori's note, and his cell phone. For months she'd filled his mind during the day and graced his dreams at night. But lately the dreams had turned to nightmares filled with darkness, haunting doubts, and pain—deep, raw, unexplainable pain. His hip throbbed in response, as though he'd wrestled with the devil, or maybe like Jacob, with God.

He picked up the phone. He and Lori had played phone tag a time or two since that initial meeting and subsequent call, but God had blocked any actual connection between them. He glanced down at the paper with her number. His fingers itched to punch in the digits.

His spirit insisted he not.

Rafe knew there were consequences for disobedience, so instead of dialing her number, he brought up the last message she left him and listened, content to hear her voice.

His heart trembled.

He scrolled back through the others, replayed each one. His body heated then chilled. Emotions warred in his soul, and he knew he wrestled not with flesh and blood but with powers and principalities of darkness.

"God, I don't know what's going on here, but I do know she's in trouble. I trust You to protect her and if she is Your will for my life, bring her back to me. It would be nice to have some sign that she's alive and well. Physically at least," he added, knowing in his heart her spirit was in grave danger.

The phone signaled a missed call. Rafe frowned. *It hadn't even rang.*

He picked it up, noticed Lori's number on the caller id. His heart skipped a thud. He punched in the numbers to retrieve his voicemail then listened to the sound of Lori's voice, slurred, and weeping and all but drowned out by background noise that made his skin crawl.

He snapped the phone shut, put her note back into the bible and buried his face in hands that shook. The warrior spirit within him rose up and began to fight for her the best way he knew how. Fervent prayers on her behalf escaped in a language only God understood.

* * *

Lori headed toward Recluse, Wyoming after another round of rodeos where the cash and prizes vaulted her to the next level of achievement. She hadn't thought of Rafe in months. Hadn't allowed herself to think of him and wouldn't indulge in useless fantasies now.

She'd made peace with the fact she was nothing more than a bad seed and there was no way around it. Oh, she tried to be good. She stayed out of the bars for weeks on end, attended the prayer services before or after each rodeo when available, even visited with a group of supposedly devout believers who traveled a state-wide circuit within the national itinerary, but nothing seemed to help or make an impact on her life.

Nor had she found the support she'd hoped, only judgment and criticism. Answers to her questions only incited debates until she was scorned for her doubt and unbelief or shunned completely. Maverick was right when he said there was no, in between, and since she couldn't succeed at being good, Lori figured she'd be bad.

Just as she had all of her life.

More than once, she thought about calling Stanley or Amber or even Lexie for counsel, but was too ashamed to admit the total mess her life was in. She even considered quitting. Just give up and go home. But she was too close to making pro status, too close to the culmination of the dream that began in her heart nearly four years ago.

A dream she once thought came as a directive from God.

Now, she knew better.

God didn't give success to losers; the devil lured them into it then left them to their own devices no matter how hard they tried to be good. Besides, even at her *best*, there was no way she'd ever be good enough for a preacher.

A familiar sense of shame washed over her, but she shook off the dark thoughts with determination. The only thing that mattered now was winning the event she'd forfeited the last time she was here. One more victory would push her into professional status and enable her to join the ranks of pro rodeo riders. Maybe then she would find meaning and purpose for her existence or at least the cowboy of her dreams.

She arrived at the campground, unhitched her trailer, and turned Solomon loose in the corral, then headed straight to the Wild Horse Saloon knowing only one way to numb the pain in her heart and ease the aching emptiness in her soul.

***

Rafe passed the campground and rode through the rows of horse and camper trailers parked there as he'd done for the past six months. *Seven months, three weeks, twelve hours, and twenty minutes.*

He ground his teeth in frustration and wondered again if Lori would ever come back. The thought of her had plagued him constantly. He'd even considered a trip to Bandera, had gone so far as to call information and find her father's name and phone number as well as the location of the Bar S ranch. He mapped the distance and knew exactly how long it would take him to drive to Bandera or fly into San Antonio and rent a car.

But something in his spirit always stopped him and though he knew he couldn't pursue her, not once had he failed to pray for her—her safety and her soul.

He turned the last curve and his breath lodged in his throat at the white luxury coach parked at the very end of the row. He knew it belonged to her even before he noted *Bar S, Bandera, TX* inscribed on the side, with her and Solomon's name beneath. His heart comprehended and lifted to the tune of a happy beat. He stopped his truck alongside the trailer, climbed out and then knocked on the door of the living quarters.

"She ain't there."

Jed's voice grated on his nerves quicker than a rake on concrete. He turned. "Do you know where she is?"

He leered, chuckled. "Sure do, over at the Wild Horse having a grand old time."

Rafe's heart plunged into his stomach. His disappointment must have shown because Jed doubled over with laughter.

"Got it bad, huh preacher man? Well, your little filly is over at the bar, shaking her tail for the whole world to see and tempting every cowboy in the place."

Rafe turned on his heel, slammed into his truck and roared away, throwing dust and gravel in his wake. He swerved into the parking lot of the Wild Horse Saloon, parked his truck and stomped up to the door. He hesitated at the entrance, looked in and saw her. The slow, suggestive moves she executed via table-top while her lips moved to the tune on the jukebox set fire to his blood. Emotions pumped through him—base, primeval, and fiercely possessive.

The music stopped. She turned. Their eyes met.

The beer bottle dropped from her fingers. Everyone turned to see what happened. Silence ensued.

Rafe walked through the swinging doors and up to the table then extended a hand toward her. She hesitated but a moment, then with eyes lowered and a dark flush on her cheeks, placed her fingers in his palm. He helped her down and turned to lead her from the building only to be met at the door by Jed.

"Hey little lady, preacher man bothering you?"

She shook her head.

Jed slid his arm around her waist. "Why don't you send him packing and we'll have ourselves a good old time."

She stiffened and leaned into Rafe. "Back off, Jed, or you're gonna think hell done showed up," he warned and twirled her away from the man's lecherous paws.

Jed stepped in front of them. "Let the little lady speak for herself."

Rafe let her go, looked down at her. "You want to stay with him?"

She shook her head again.

Jed slid between them. "Speak up, sweetheart we can't hear your brains rattle."

She stepped away from him and lifted a wary gaze to Rafe's. "I want to leave."

"You heard her," Rafe said and shoved his way between them.

Jed side-stepped Rafe and grabbed her by the arm. "C'mon, sweetheart, you'll have much more fun with me than with the preacher here."

Rafe turned on his heel and shoved her behind him. His fist connected with Jed's jaw in a resounding *thwack* and the man landed in a heap on the ground. "I told you to back off."

Jed bellowed and lunged to his feet. His arms wrapped like steel manacles around Rafe's waist and the two tumbled. Punches flew. The sound of fists on flesh accentuated by grunts of pain rent the air.

"Stop it!" Lori screamed. "Somebody help before he gets hurt!"

A man rushed over to separate the two scrappers. He shook them loose and stood between them. Shock widened his eyes.

"Rafe?"

Rafe looked at the surprise on Bud Jackson's face and grimaced. He flexed his fist then shook out his hand. Blood and dirt covered his knuckles. His right eye was swollen shut, his lip busted. Jed was in worse shape than he with two black eyes and a broken nose. Humiliation crept up his neck and heated his cheeks. He ducked his head and muttered, "Sorry," then reached a hand down to help Jed up.

Jed spit out a curse and rolled away then staggered to his feet and stumbled off.

Rafe turned and limped toward his truck.

"Wait!" Lori cried and ran after him. "Rafe, wait."

He turned on her in an angry whirl, groaned when his bad leg nearly buckled beneath him. He clutched the tailgate to steady himself and gritted his teeth against the pain, physical and emotional. "Go home, Lori."

"But..."

He shook his head, fumbled his way to the door, climbed into the vehicle, and drove off.

Chapter Ten

Lori stood in the dust trail of Rafe's truck and watched him drive away. Tears streamed down her cheeks when she realized her worst nightmare had just materialized. Burned away by Maverick's words, her own jaded experience, and her recent shoot to stardom, any thoughts she'd entertained of changing her wanton ways had flown out the window like so much dirty grease. Women and girls envied her, cowboys wanted her. She was at the top of her form...wealthy, adored...and lured into the lusts of the flesh by the glitz and glamour of success.

Again.

Guess what she'd felt for Rafe so many months ago had been no more than infatuation.

Then why did she hurt so?

She flinched when a gentle hand touched her shoulder. "Are you all right, missy? Can I take you somewhere?"

The man who had separated Rafe and Jed stood before her. Concern etched his tanned face and lit his topaz eyes to golden flames. She burst into tears. He hauled her against his huge barrel of a chest and held her in a fatherly embrace.

"I've ruined everything," she mumbled between sobs. "He hates me for sure."

The rock-solid muscles beneath her cheek vibrated as laughter rumbled from the man. "Oh, honey, only one thing will make a man like Rafe Judson fight over a woman and it certainly ain't hate. He may be angry for a while and I'm sure embarrassed as all get out, but hatred is one thing the man ain't capable of feeling. I know him well enough to assure you of that."

"How long have you known him?" She mumbled into his chest then brushed her eyes with her sleeve and buried her face against him once more.

"Met him the night of his accident. That old bull changed his life and since, Rafe has changed mine."

Lori moved out of his embrace and gazed up at him. "Will you tell me about him?"

The gentleman offered his arm and patted her hand when she curled hers through it.

"Anything you want to know, sweetheart," he answered and led her next door to the Wildflower Café.

They sat in strained silence until a waitress appeared with water glasses and coffee cups filled to the brim.

"Would you like something to eat?" he asked.

Lori shook her head. "No thanks. Coffee is fine."

"What's your name?"

Lori pulled a couple of napkins out of the holder and wiped her eyes then muttered her name.

"So, you're the one," he said, a hint of awe in his voice.

Her head jerked up, eyes widened. "I beg your pardon."

A soft chuckle escaped the barreled chest. "Rafe told me months ago he was tied up in knots over a woman, though he never mentioned your name. The ruckus he just indulged in can only mean one thing—he ain't untied yet."

"You said you met him the night of his accident?"

He nodded. "Yep and that's one night this old cowboy will never forget. Right here in Recluse, nearly four years ago now. I'd followed his career for years and was thrilled when the PBR accepted our bid to have the rodeo come here. They'd always turned us down, you see, said we were too small, and no pro bull rider wants to compete in a town few people ever heard of. An answer to prayer is what it was 'cause that rodeo brought more than recognition to us. The money it brought in practically saved us from fading away into a ghost town."

The waitress appeared to refill their cups and offer pie or some other desert to go with the coffee. Lori declined with a shake of her head and waited for the waitress to leave before addressing the man seated across from her again. "So, what happened, how did Rafe change your life, Mr. ... I'm sorry I never asked your name."

"Name's Bud Jackson, honey, and I guess it wasn't Rafe exactly what changed my life, but God working in and through him that did. I was emcee back then, same as I am now. Rafe had been number one for as long as I can remember, his career phenomenal, and we were ecstatic to have him here. Despite the good hosting the rodeo brought to Recluse, everything about that night was all wrong. The bulls were meaner 'n hell..." His voice trailed off. A flush climbed up his neck.

"Sorry for the language, missy."

Lori smiled at the disjointed English and chopped sentences of the dark-haired, golden-eyed man and waved the apology away with a shake of her head and hand.

Bud cleared his throat. "Anyway, the bulls were the meanest I'd ever seen, and I'd never seen so many injured cowboys in one event. The crowd loved it—they cheered and chanted for Rafe, but all evening I'd had this weird feeling that he shouldn't ride. I searched him out and tried to convince him not to. The bull he'd pulled was a known killer. But he wouldn't listen. He was cold back then, cold and hard. Never saw such deadness in a man's eyes."

A visible shudder shook Bud. He lifted the cup to his lips with a shaking hand. Lori felt her own tighten around the mug of bitter brew sitting in front of her. Her heart thundered in her chest, but she kept quiet and anticipated the rest of the story. She listened with mounting horror as Bud recalled the accident with vivid clarity. The blood drained from her face.

"Oh, my word, he *is* lucky to be alive."

Bud nodded. "Stayed in a coma for right near two months and if seeing that miracle wasn't enough to change my sorry life, watching him grow from the cold, hard, bitter man he was to the man he is today sure has."

"What do you mean?" Lori asked.

Bud eyed her a moment then smiled. "Deep calls unto deep, missy. The reason I knew Rafe was a cold, hard, bitter man back then is because I was once one, too. My life had been down the sewer on more than one occasion.

"You name it, I done it. I'd started the steady climb, or should I say unsteady climb, out of the last shi...er...uh...hole...uh...outhouse," his words trailed off, skin turned several shades of red. He took a gulp of coffee then coughed and sputtered as though the liquid scalded his throat.

"Sorry," He stammered at Lori, swallowed a guzzle of water, and then rolled his eyes heavenward. "I'm working on the language, Lord, but thank You for the help."

Lori burst into a fit of giggles. Bud's bellow of laughter followed until tears streamed down their cheeks.

"Whew!" he said once sanity was restored between them.

Lori grinned and took a sip of coffee.

Bud chuckled and did the same. "Anyway, while Rafe was in that coma I made peace with God and somehow, somewhere along the road of his recovery, so did he. We've been best friends ever since."

"He'll probably never speak to me again."

Bud rose from his seat, dropped a few dollars on the table to pay their tab, and reached a hand to help her up. "I'm not so sure about that. Give him time, honey and in the mean while, you might consider making peace with God yourself."

"How do you do that, Mr. Jackson, what's the key?"

Bud gave her a tender smile. "Redemption."

"Will you visit with me again and tell me more about Rafe?"

Bud nodded. "I'll see you tomorrow. Now, how about I drive you back to your trailer?"

On impulse, Lori turned and gave him a hug then whispered, "Thank you."

* * *

Rafe avoided the campgrounds until Saturday evening. He awoke more than once the past two nights in a cold sweat, shuddering from dreams he couldn't remember but with sensations and memories assailing him—gut-wrenching fear, rippling pain, total darkness. He tried to shut out the feelings and rest but every time he closed his eyes, his heart raced, and muscles tensed until he ached all over and he did the only thing he could think of, the only thing that brought peace: *Pray.*

He'd said more prayers and done more reparation and soul searching in the past couple of days than he had since his conversion three years ago. What he found, he abhorred. Hard to face the fact that no matter how much you love the Lord, sin resides in the flesh.

Even for a preacher.

Anger, lust, and pride lie dormant until you think you've mastered your baser instincts then rise up when least expected.

He talked to few people since his skirmish with Jed on Thursday. Bud had been about his only guest, and he worried his pews would be empty come Sunday. He made his way to the arena and announcers box with a mixture of anticipation and trepidation. He had no idea if Lori stayed in town, if she would ride tonight, or if he'd discover her drunk or worse, drunk, *and* dancing on another table. His heart cringed at the thought.

She was one thing he hadn't come to terms with—within himself or with the Lord.

He made his way to the announcers' box, engaged in the familiar banter, and waited for his turn to speak. When Bud placed the microphone in his hand, Rafe cleared his throat. "Before I ask the Lord's blessings on the event and everyone here, I must ask your forgiveness. Some of you may know about the fight I engaged in Thursday evening with one of my oldest rivals..."

His words trailed off when a voice rang out from the crowd asking who won.

He swallowed a chuckle, bit back a smile and cleared his throat again. "We won't go into details on why, wherefore, and who won. Let's suffice it to say I deeply regret the incident and apologize to all who witnessed the fracas. Jed, old buddy if you're here, I'm sorry. Let's talk."

Elation swept through him at the response of the crowd. When the cheers and whistles died down, he prayed, and then left the box and headed down to the pens. Jed met him about halfway.

"Guess confrontation between us has been long overdue, hasn't it, Rafe?"

Rafe put his hand on Jed's shoulder. "Yeah, it has. But things don't have to remain as they are, Jed. Can you forgive me?"

"Forgive you for what, always being better than me in the bullring or that you got all the prettiest girls? For the fame, fortune and success I craved but you achieved?" Jed shook his head and emitted a sad little chuckle.

"It's taken me a long time to come to grips with the truth that you're a better man all around than I could ever dream of being. I wasn't raised to be this way. Guess all the years of competition and failure just got the best of me. Your beating helped me put things in perspective." He grinned then sobered. "I'm the one who needs forgiveness."

Rafe gave Jed's shoulder an affectionate squeeze. "No one man is better than the other. We're all created equal in God's eyes. I'm sure you have untold qualities and scores of untapped potential. Let's just wipe the slate clean and start over, shall we?"

Jed nodded his agreement, lowered his voice a notch. "For what it's worth, I never slept with your girlfriend."

Rafe's heart did a happy little flip at the news. "It's worth a whole lot, Jed. Thank you. See you in church tomorrow?"

Jed grinned, relief and peace evident on his face.

"You just might at that, preacher man," he said with a chuckle.

The two parted ways just as Lori's name blared over the intercom. Rafe walked over to the arena as she shot out of the chute and rounded the barrels in one of the fastest and smoothest exhibitions he'd ever seen. He cheered her success along with the crowd but ducked away when she left the arena. He didn't want to talk to her yet, couldn't. His heart was too unsettled.

Sunday morning dawned bright and clear. Rafe spent his usual pre-service prayer time pacing the floors in his tiny house. He'd been up and down all night, wrestling with his desire to go to Lori and wrap her in his love. He prayed for her instead. His sermon that morning was on how the lusts of the flesh warred with the desire of the spirit and how love and forgiveness were the only antidotes to anger and wrath. His altar call was one of the largest he'd received since he began serving the members of Cowboy Up Church two years ago.

Though he never made eye contact, he knew when Lori entered the building. He felt her presence. His heart leapt, spirit rejoiced. By the time service was complete and the crowd dispersed, he left in search of her. He drove to the campground to no avail, she was no where to be found.

Chapter Eleven

His words devastated her.

Lori left the campground and headed home with tears on her cheeks and agony in her heart. She had no idea why she even set foot in church this morning. Only that she wanted to see Rafe one last time. She'd seen the passion on his face and heard the conviction in his voice when he talked of grace and mercy, of love and forgiveness, but didn't think his words were directed to her. How could he forgive her when she couldn't forgive herself?

She doubted even God would forgive her.

Meant to convict yet encourage and heal, his words pricked her conscience, pierced her heart, and scraped her soul until only guilt and condemnation remained. She pulled off the highway more than once to weep and arrived in Bandera filled with regret and remorse. All of her success including the win Saturday night meant little to her now.

Nothing mattered anymore.

She drove up to the barn and unloaded her horse then unhitched the trailer, glad her parents were away on vacation. Even more grateful they hadn't met up with her as planned before the rodeo. She'd have a few days to herself to figure out what to do with the rest of her life.

Or whether to end it.

Instead of frightening, the dark thought enticed. A shiver shook her. Ideas assaulted her…Could she do it? How? Where? How would it affect her parents? Would they get over the grief to find relief in the fact she wouldn't be around to bring more misery to their lives? Or would her choice kill them too? Her heart cringed at the thought.

She entered the house, made her way into her bedroom and turned on the radio to combat the vortex of thoughts in her head then decided to take a shower. She stood a long time in hopes the hot, pulsating spray would drown the voices that vied for and against her early demise. When the water ran tepid she turned off the faucet, wrapped her hair in a towel and body in a thick, terrycloth robe then sat at the vanity table in her room.

One look in the mirror and she burst into tears. A few minutes later she heard footsteps in the kitchen and Stanley's voice call her name. She shook out her hair, dried her eyes and rushed to the door.

"I'll be out in a minute; I just got out of the shower!" she called and closed it. She hurried into clean clothes and splashed cold water on her face but couldn't hide the evidence of her emotional state. She sat back at the vanity table, sprayed conditioner on her hair, and worked the tangles out of her golden locks with a wide-tooth comb. A knock sounded. Lori bid his entrance and turned when Stanley pushed the door open but didn't enter.

"What are you doing here?"

He leaned on the door frame. "I told your father I'd keep an eye on the place while they were gone. I saw your truck and knew you were back. I knocked on the back door and worried when you didn't answer. I used my key to come in and check on you. Are you all right?"

One glance at the concern on his face and she fell apart. She tossed down the comb, rushed to where he stood, threw herself in his arms, and confessed all. She told him about Rafe and divulged every sordid detail of her life up to that moment. She revealed her darkest secrets and disclosed the internal debate she'd had on whether or not she should just put an end all to the misery she caused herself and others.

He stroked her back and shoulders in a caress meant to soothe. "That's not the answer, Lori. Suicide never is."

"Then what is the answer, Stanley?"

He shifted her in his embrace, cupped her face in his hands, and brushed the tears off her cheeks with his thumbs. "Redemption."

She searched his gaze for condemnation, found love and compassion instead. "Is there any hope for redemption after all I've done?"

"It's never too late for redemption—for anyone, regardless of what they've done. You'll come to the house for the next few days. I'll wait while you pack a bag."

Relief swept through her that she wouldn't be alone to wrestle with the demons in her heart and mind. "Are you sure Amber won't mind?"

He chuckled. "You know she won't. She'd probably kick my sorry carcass all the way back over here when she discovered I'd left you alone in this condition."

Lori giggled. He hugged her again then moved her out of his embrace. Gathering up her courage she asked, "How do you find redemption, Stan? I've tried, really, but nothing seemed to change."

He eyed her with a tender smile and brushed the hair off her face. "You can't find redemption, Lors. You can't earn it or buy it, either. Like forgiveness, grace, and mercy, redemption is a gift. You only have to receive it. You've been raised in church, you should know this."

"Then what's wrong with me? Why can't I seem to get it right? What's the key?"

Lori knew by the way he closed his eyes and hesitated, Stanley prayed for wisdom, guidance, and direction, so she tamped down the impatience within. When he looked at her again, she knew he had the answers she sought.

"There is nothing wrong with you, per-se', Lori. Faith is a heart issue. What you need to consider is why you want redemption. What are your motives? God wants us to love Him and come to Him and receive Him because of Who He is, and He loves you just as you are. Seeking redemption for any reason other than to be in right standing with God is not going to work.

"Now, once that is your true motive, the key is to surrender your will for His, and to receive and welcome His lordship over your life then receive His goodness as your own. Things won't change overnight, Lori, but if you stay faithful to what He shows you, and tells you, your life will be filled with such peace, that the pace of change won't matter. Now, get your things together and I'll give your father a call."

Fear curled through Lori. "Please don't tell him all this."

A soft smile curved Stanley's mouth. "I wouldn't dream of betraying your confidence and worrying him for no reason."

"Thank you," she whispered.

* * *

Rafe pulled into the parking lot of the Wildflower Café about as exhausted as a man could get. For three days he wrestled with himself and argued with God over what he should do about Lori. What he wanted was to run after her, follow to the ends of the earth if necessary, and wrap her in his love. More than anything he longed to shower her with affection and mercy and grace until she understood how precious she was in God's sight and in his. What he had to do was wait. Wait on the Lord and submit to His leading, His guidance, and His direction.

Rafe knew God worked behind the scenes and if he disobeyed and followed his own agenda, he'd only interfere with the process of God reaching down and lifting His daughter out of the muck and mire of sin, out of the pits of hell, and establishing her on the rock of salvation.

But all the knowledge in the world didn't stop the longing. Or the frustration.

He slammed out of his truck, stomped into the café, and slid into a booth. The waitress brought coffee, water, and silverware.

"Morning, the usual breakfast fare or are you ready for lunch?"

Rafe sipped the coffee and sighed. "The usual is fine, thanks, still a bit too early for lunch."

She moseyed toward the kitchen to place his order, refilling coffee cups along the way. Rafe closed his eyes and sent another silent plea to God for Lori and for peace of mind to calm the storm of emotions within his heart and soul. The conversation between the couple in the booth behind him snagged his attention.

"I wish we'd headed home the moment Stanley called," the woman said.

The gentleman heaved a sigh. "Why? You know he's got things under control. Everything will be fine. We've never been to Colorado, and I'd love to see a bit of it while we're here."

"I know, but I'm worried about Lori."

Rafe's ears perked up. *Lori? It couldn't be.....*

The gentleman's voice continued, "I'd love to know how she did Saturday night."

"*I'd* love to know what upset her. How can you be concerned about the rodeo and not your daughter's wellbeing?"

"Now sweetheart," the man's tone resembled that of an extremely patient person. "You know Stanley took her home with him. He won't let anything happen to Lori. She'll be fine."

The lady harrumphed. "I'm still worried."

The gentleman chuckled. "That's what you do best."

Rafe grinned. "Thank you, God," he whispered. He rose from his seat, turned around and came face to face with Lori's father. There was no mistaking the resemblance between the two, especially those dark brown eyes.

"Excuse me, I didn't mean to eavesdrop but couldn't help but overhear your conversation. You wouldn't happen to be Mr. and Mrs. Strickland, would you?"

The fellow's eyes widened in recognition, he sprang from the booth and extended a hand toward Rafe. "Rafe Judson. I'd know you anywhere. Yes, I'm Roy Strickland and this is my wife, Mary."

Rafe shook the proffered hand and tipped his hat to Lori's mother.

"Please join us," Roy offered. "Mary, come sit next to me, darling, so Mr. Judson can sit there."

Mary murmured her agreement and hurried to move into the seat her husband had occupied moments earlier.

Rafe grabbed his cup of coffee and slid into the booth as Roy sat. "To answer your question, Lori won the barrel racing by a longshot. That is one well-bred, superbly trained animal she has. Did you raise him?"

A rumble of laughter shook Mary. She arched an eyebrow at Rafe, her features alight with mirth. "You just stepped in it, cowboy."

Roy chuckled at his wife's teasing. "No, we didn't raise Solomon. Our longtime friend, and horseman extraordinaire, Stanley Morrison did. That boy is going to run me out of business yet."

The laughter in his tone belied the words. Rafe grinned and listened while her parents talked of Lori and the young man both thought of as the son they never had.

Chapter Twelve

Lori spent the next several days wrapped in the love of her friends. With the kindness, consideration, and counsel of Amber and Stanley as well as the delight she found in their children and extended family whom she'd known forever, she rediscovered the joy of life.

On Sunday she attended services at the church she'd grown up in. She sat in the pew her family had occupied for generations, waiting...praying for a word from God—word of hope, or a hint of peace, direction, or clarity.

Lori's attention was drawn away from the open bible she held and the praise music coming from the choir loft when Lexie Harris slid in beside her.

"Hey, Lori," she whispered.

Lori smiled. "I didn't know you came to services here."

Lexie shook her head. "Normally I don't. I haven't found a church home yet. I sometimes attend Mass but for some reason, tonight I felt the Lord urging me here. I hope you don't mind me joining you."

Lori smiled again. "Not at all, in fact, I'm glad you're here." A pause in the music indicated the service was about to begin. She and Lexie stood as the pastor arrived in his place behind the podium on the altar.

"Love is not selfish or self centered," he began. "It is not boastful or rude. Love does not seek after its own agenda but seeks the way of the Lord."

Conviction stabbed Lori's heart. *Oh God, I've been all of those things and more, behaved that way my entire life.* She searched her heart but couldn't find a moment when she'd thought of anyone beside herself. The tears started, slow at first then poured from her eyes as the words of First Corinthians Thirteen hammered home. She felt Lexie's arm go around her as the pastor finished his message, his words almost the same she'd heard from Rafe a week ago.

"If you are away from God, need to repent or recommit your life to Him, come now. Congregation, please keep your eyes closed and pray as folks come to Jesus."

"Do you want to go up?" Lexie whispered. "I'll go with you if you want."

Sobs shook her so hard she couldn't speak so Lori nodded.

The two made their way to the altar where, at last, Lori made peace with God and found the redemption she'd sought for so long, but in all the wrong ways and with all the wrong motives.

Later, she sat on the front porch of the Morrison's' house and gazed at the star-filled sky. A huge yellow moon hung in the heavens like a golden pearl. The gentle breeze whispered comfort and peace to her battered heart and weary soul. She heard the voice of God's spirit call, wooing her into a level of intimacy she'd yet to experience. In fact, one she'd run from in search of the illusive soul mate, the cowboy of her dreams.

In the silence of the night, she opened her heart and mind and surrendered her spirit and life to His plan and for the first time in her life felt the very real presence of God and with that, the peace that surpasses all understanding.

Stanley walked out on the porch and settled beside her on the swing. "How are you?" he asked and slid his arm around her.

She sighed and rested her head on his shoulder. "I'm ready to go home, Stanley. The battle is over. God has won. I'll never go back to the life I led. I may return to rodeo, but never again will I fall victim to the lies that success and stardom much less booze, drugs, or sex can satisfy the empty space only God can fill."

He brushed his lips over her forehead. "Good to hear. Your father called."

"Where are they?"

"They'll be home tomorrow night. I'll take you back Tuesday morning."

She snuggled against him. "Thank you for being such a wonderful friend, more than a friend but a brother, to me all these years. You're still the best."

Amber walked out and they made room on the swing. Lori turned to her. "And thank you for being the best friend a foolish young girl could ever ask for."

Amber laughed and hugged her. "You're welcome, but I'm never going to toss Stanley out so you can take him off my hands."

Lori giggled at the familiar joke between them. "Better not, because there's not another cowboy like him in this world."

Amber cuddled her as she would a younger sister.

"Yes there is. Your cowboy will show up when the time is right. God will lead him to you."

"I hope so," she sighed but her heart ached with fear that she'd already ruined the love of a lifetime with Rafe.

Amber and Stanley said goodnight and went inside, but Lori stayed out a while longer and marveled at how much her life had changed in one short week. She found it ironic her lowest point occurred days before Halloween and her highest only weeks away from Thanksgiving. The upcoming holiday season lay before her like an unwrapped gift, full of surprise, sparkling with promise. *I've so much to be thankful for.* Her heart overflowed with praise for the goodness of God.

As usual, her thoughts circled back to Rafe. She recalled the conversations she'd had with Bud Jackson and what he told her—how Rafe had been raised by his single mother and took up bull riding shortly before her death. After which, his life became a rollercoaster of success and failure and fame and fortune until the time of his accident.

Their lives, so different yet parallel surprised her. Where she had everything a girl could ask for, he'd been poor, but both were never satisfied with their lot in life. She remembered Bud's recollection of Rafe's conversion and how he determined to be the best cowboy preacher God could ask for. She wondered how he was doing, if he thought about her at all and if he could ever forgive her. Should she seek him out or wait and see what God had in store?

Would she ever get over him?

The next morning after Stanley fed the horses and she shared breakfast with him and his family, he put her overnight bag in his truck, and they drove to her house. Anticipation danced in her heart, and she looked forward to the opportunity to renew and strengthen the bond with her parents. Her father would be so happy to find she pondered the thought of returning to college.

If only she could figure out what God wanted for her life, His plan for her future.

When Stan turned in the drive and they neared the house, her heart plunged into her stomach then soared upward and jumped into a thunderous rhythm. She gasped and reached for his hand.

"What is it?"

She tilted her head toward a vehicle parked in the drive. "That's Rafe's truck. Why do you suppose he's here?"

Stanley chuckled. "Well, you can bet he didn't drive more than twenty hours just to chew you out."

* * *

Rafe sat at the kitchen table with Lori's father and listened while he rattled on about everything...the weather, his ranch, his daughter. That Roy doted on Lori warmed his heart. He'd never had the love of a father, didn't even know who the man was. His mother had died with the secret in her heart. The only thing he knew about the man who'd sired him was that he hadn't loved his mother enough to stick by her when she told him she carried his child. He continued his life as rodeo rookie and died in an accident shortly thereafter.

Mrs. Strickland refreshed his coffee and pulled Rafe's thoughts from their wanderings.

After their meeting at the Wildflower Café Wednesday morning, they checked into a B&B then attended evening services at Cowboy Up Church. Rafe spent the next two days talking with them. He told them what had happened with Lori and how he felt about her. When Roy suggested he follow them home Rafe declined because of Sunday services. However, he left right after and drove straight through, stopping when absolutely necessary to stretch his legs or catch a few winks.

He'd arrived thirty-minutes ago to find she wasn't home yet. She'd spent the last week at their friend's neighboring ranch and would return sometime after breakfast. The sound of an approaching vehicle then doors opening and closing drew their attention.

"Bet that's them right now," Roy said and rose from his chair.

Rafe did the same and followed him outside just as Lori and her companion started toward the house. She hesitated, their eyes met. A kaleidoscope of emotions skittered across her features...a flush of pleasure, a hint of fear, a glimmer of hope.

"Lori, darling, look who's here," her father said then continued speaking before she could comment. "Stanley my boy, how's it going? Meet Rafe Judson."

Stanley put Lori's bag down and offered his hand. "Heard a lot about you."

Rafe shook the proffered hand and nodded. "As I have of you. All good." He glanced at Lori then back to Stanley. "I hope."

Stan chuckled and picked up the bag again. "Most of it. How about a cup of coffee, Roy?"

Roy opened the door and waited for him to enter. "Sure, come on in. Shall I pour you another cup Rafe, and one for you, Lori?"

"We'll be in shortly, Daddy."

She lifted her gaze to his and Rafe's heart leapt at what he saw there. Hope. Peace. Love.

Redemption.

"Can you ever forgive me, Rafe?"

He cupped her cheek in one hand, ran the other through her thick, golden locks then pulled her in his arms. With a laugh he picked her up and twirled her around.

"Only if you agree to marry me," he whispered before his mouth covered hers in a kiss designed to banish the slightest trace of doubt from her decadent chocolate eyes.

Dear Readers,

If you're familiar with my **Tempered** series, you'll recognize Lori from book 3, <u>Tempered Fire</u>. Back then she was a spoiled, little rich girl used to getting what she wanted—wild, rebellious, and totally dissatisfied with her lot in life.

Aren't we all like that to some degree?

Even though the bible exhorts us to learn to be content in all circumstances, and in *ALL* things to give God praise, we whine and complain, never truly satisfied.

Like many of us, Lori sought happiness in vices such as booze, drugs and sex—and like most, ended up emptier than ever. And, like many in turmoil of whatever kind and degree, wondered if there IS blessed relief in suicide. I know I've been there myself more than once when the circumstances in life seem too difficult to bear.

So, what's the answer?

Redemption.

Redemption and trust even when you don't understand why God allowed that particular turn in the road on your journey of life.

Many find redemption and rejoice in their salvation then return to the same destructive patterns—if not in deed, in attitude.

How *does* one break free of the bondage of negativity?

W. Clement Stone said, "Whatever the mind can conceive, it can achieve."

Envision your life the way you want it to be then call those things (the circumstances in your life) that be not, as though they are! By believing in your heart and confessing with your mouth you work out your salvation and open yourself to receive the blessings God has in store for you. —Try it, it works!

It is my prayer that if you don't already know Him, you'll seek Jesus as your Lord and Savior and if you do know Him, you'll pursue a closer walk with Him.

Until later take care, God Bless and remember.... Don't allow the world outside and around you to poison the beauty within.

Pamela S Thibodeaux

"Inspirational with an Edge!" ™

THANK YOU!

I pray you've been blessed as I have by your purchase of this book. If you've **enjoyed Lori's Redemption** please write a positive review and post it at online retailers (Amazon, B&N, Kobo, iBooks, etc.) and websites where readers gather and/or your social media platforms (FaceBook, Good Reads, BookBub, Twitter, etc).

About the Author

Pamela S. Thibodeaux grew up in the town of Iowa, Louisiana. She is a mother, grandmother and deeply committed Christian who firmly believes in God and His promises.

"God is very real to me, and I feel that people today need and want to hear more of His truths wherever they can glean them. People are hungry for practical (and real) Christian values, not some 'holier-than-thou' beliefs that are impossible to believe and impossible to live up to," Pamela says.

"I do my best to encourage readers to develop a personal relationship with God. The deepest desire of my heart is to glorify God and to get His message of faith, trust and forgiveness to a hurting world."

Email Pamela at: pam@pamelathibodeaux.com
Visit her website: http://www.pamelathibodeaux.com
Or blog: http://pamswildroseblog.blogspot.com

Sign up to receive **_Pam's Newsletter_** and get a FREE short story.

Other Titles by
Pamela S Thibodeaux

My Heart Weeps

After thirty years married to the man of her dreams, Melena Rhyker is devastated by her husband's death. Relief comes in the form of an artist's retreat at the Crossed Penn ranch in Utopia, TX. She rediscovers a forgotten dream as her artistic talent flourishes into that of a gallery-worthy artist. Will she have the courage to follow the path she was destined to travel?

Garrett Saunders has been on the run most of his life. Abused and abandoned as a child, he escapes the clutches of a past filled with pain and shame and hides from his calling as a Native American healer. His years as a CIA agent aid in overcoming his childhood and honing his talent and skill as a fine art photographer.

Follow their journey as two people who come from totally different backgrounds, but share gifts of gigantic proportions, find meaning and purpose in the Texas Hill Country.

Keri's Christmas Wish

For as long as she can remember, Keri Jackson has despised the hype and commercialism around Christmas so much she seldom enjoys the holiday. Will she get her wish and be free of the angst to truly enjoy Christmas this year?

A devout Christian at heart, Jeremy Hinton, a Psychotherapist, Life Coach, Spiritual Mentor and Energy Medicine Practitioner has studied all of the world's religions and homeopathic healing modalities. But when a rare bacterial infection threatens the life of the woman he loves, will all of his faith and training be for naught?

Love is a Rose (Devotional): Music is the magical entry into the spirit world; the golden gate into the Kingdom of God. But we mustn't be of the mindset that God only uses Christian music to reach out and touch our mind, heart and spirit. God uses *any* and **every** means available to speak to His children.

Our job is to be open and receptive.

In this devotional, Pamela S Thibodeaux shares how God opened her spirit to a deeper understanding of the abundance of His grace and mercy through the words of the song, *The Rose* sung by Country & Western artist Conway Twitty.

Pamela offers *Seeds to Ponder* and a prayer as she parallels the love of God and the Christian life to each verse of the song.

Set at the tail end of the Vietnam War era, ***Circles of Fate*** takes the reader from Fort Benning, Georgia to Thibodaux, Louisiana. A romantic saga, this gripping novel covers nearly twenty years in the lives of Shaunna Chatman and Todd Jameson. Constantly thrown together and torn apart by fate, the two are repeatedly forced to choose between love and duty, right and wrong, standing on faith or succumbing to the world's viewpoint on life, love, marriage and fidelity. With intriguing twists and turns, fate brings together a cast of characters whose lives will forever be entwined. Through it all is the hand of God as He works all things together for the good of those who love Him and are called according to His purpose.

A visionary is someone who sees into the future Taylor Forrestier sees into the past but only as it pertains to her work. Hailed by her peers as *"a visionary with an instinct for beauty and an eye for the unique"* Taylor is undoubtedly a brilliant architect and gifted designer. But she and twin brother Trevor, share more than a successful business. The two share a childhood wrought with lies and deceit and the kind of abuse that's disgustingly prevalent in today's society. Can the love of God and the awesome healing power of His grace and mercy free the twins from their past and open their hearts to the good plan and the future He has for their lives? Find out in ***The Visionary*** ~ Where the awesome power of God's love heals the most wounded of souls.

The Inheritance *is about the chance we all long for...the chance to start over.* Widowed at age thirty-nine and suffering from empty nest syndrome, Rebecca Sinclair is overshadowed by grief and loneliness. Her husband has been deceased for a year, her oldest child has moved to New York in pursuit of an acting career and her youngest child is attending college in France. Having spent over half of her life as a wife and mother, she has no idea what God has in store for her now. Will an unexpected inheritance in the wine country of New York bring meaning and purpose to her life and give her the courage to love again?

US Postal worker Raymond Jacobey has been in love with the little widow since he first set eyes on her. A wanderer searching for the ever-illusive soul mate, Ray has never stayed in one place too long. Raised by self-centered, high-power executives, he's longed for the idyllic life of residing in a cozy house in a small town with the love of his life. Will he gain the heart of the lovely widow, or will he lose her to the wine country of New York?

Tempered Hearts: Rancher Craig Harris and veterinarian Tamera Collins clash from the moment they meet. Innocence is pitted against arrogance as tempers rise and passions ignite to form a love as pure as the finest gold, fresh from the crucible and as strong as steel. Thrown together amid tragedy and unsated passion, Tamera and Craig share a strong attraction that neither accepts as the first stages of love. Torn between desire and dislike, they must make peace with their pasts and God in order to open up to the love blossoming between them. It is a love that nothing can destroy when they come to understand that *only when hearts are tempered, minds are opened, and wills are softened can man discern the will of God for his life.*

Dr. Scott Hensley (introduced in *Tempered Hearts*) has built a wall around his heart since the death of his wife and parents. Katrina Simmons is recovering from scars inflicted on her as a battered wife. Can dreams be renewed and faith strengthened? Can they find joy and peace in God's love and in love for one another? Find out in ***Tempered Dreams***.

Amber Harris is a good girl on the brink of womanhood. Stanley Morrison is a young man at the start of his life. For each other, they have always felt the fireworks that two people in love should feel. But the questions about his past, his pride, and Amber's father might be the end of what could be a strong relationship. As the two try to protect their budding romance, some unlikely but powerful forces conspire to keep them apart. Will they survive the wishes of everyone around them with their relationship intact? Find out in ***Tempered Fire.***

All around rodeo cowboy and heir to the Rockin' H Ranch, Ace Harris is determined not to fall in love. He's only loved one woman in his life, his mother, and no one can even come close to filling her boots. Lexie Morgan thinks rodeo cowboys have rocks for brains and a death wish for a soul. A broken childhood and the death of her father and best friend leave her doubting and questioning God (despite her years of religious upbringing) and afraid of love. Can two young people who clash from the onset learn to trust in the healing power of God and find love and happiness amidst tragedy and grief? Find out in ***Tempered Joy.***

Anytime is the perfect time for love.
In ***Love in Season,*** author Pamela S Thibodeaux brings together eight of her most beloved romance

stories—one for each season plus four holidays that revolve around love and family. Includes (Winter) **Winter Madness**, (Valentine's Day) **Choices**, (Spring) **Cathy's Angel**, (Easter) **Lilies for Sandi** (NEW), (Summer) **The Big Catch** (NEW), (Fall) **A Hero for Jessica**, (Thanksgiving) **Review of Love** (NEW) and (Christmas) **In His Sight**.

Sienna has survived what most succumb to - the death of a spouse and child and has maintained her faith despite her troubles. William has never met anyone who actually lived out what they say they believe. Is it true love between the faithful optimist and broody pessimist or simply *Winter Madness*? *Part of *Love in Season* collection of short stories*

Best-selling novelist and songwriter, Camie Rogers has penned numerous accounts of the secret love she holds in her heart. Country-Music Superstar Kip Allen has changed from the shy, humble boy, to the epitome of "star." Can the two rediscover each other after one night of his Home is Where the Heart is Tour? Find out in *Choices* *Part of *Love in Season* collection of short stories*

Single mom Cathy Johnson is tired of running her life alone...what she needs is a well-trained angel to help out. Jared Savoy gave up the dream of having a family when he discovered he is sterile. Can a confirmed bachelor and the mother of four find love amid normal daily chaos? Find out in *Cathy's Angel* *Part of *Love in Season* collection of short stories*

Sandi and Brett did everything backwards. They got pregnant before the wedding and had a baby instead of a honeymoon. Since, Brett has resented the fact that his dreams of a football career have been cut short and wonders how long it'll take God to forgive him for his mistakes. Sandi has played second fiddle to Brett's dreams and desires to the point of not knowing herself any longer and fears her marriage will never be a true one because of their failures. Can two hearts broken by unfulfilled dreams find healing, wholeness and restoration? Find out in *Lilies for Sandi* *Part of *Love in Season* collection of short stories*

Karla and, the love of her life, Jeff, have uncovered some uncommon ground: The Great Outdoors. For the life of her, she does not understand his love of fishing and how he can spend so much time doing so. Will she come to love the sport as much as he or will his passion for a rod and reel tangle up their relationship? Find out in ***The Big Catch*** *Part of ***Love in Season*** collection of short stories*

Anthony Paul Seville is known as the 'most eligible bachelor' in New Orleans, possibly even the entire state of Louisiana, but finds himself alone—completely and explicitly alone. Jessica Aucoin is a writer on her way to fame and fortune but is haunted by a man from her past. Will the "champion" lawyer and the author of romantic suspense find love written in their future? Find out in ***A Hero for Jessica*** *Part of ***Love in Season*** collection of short stories*

Jason Stockwell has been commissioned to interview Kylie Erickson and to review her books. Only problem is, she won't give the time of day much less an interview to someone whose type of writing she deems not worthy of respect. Can they suspend their judgmental attitudes and find true love? Find out in ***Review of Love*** *Part of ***Love in Season*** collection of short stories*

Grade-school teacher Carson Alexander has a gift— a gift that has driven a wedge between him and his family. Worse, it's put him at odds with God. Feeling alone and misunderstood, Carson views God's gift of prophecy as the worst kind of curse...that is until he meets Lorelei Conner, landscape artist extraordinaire, and perhaps the one person who may need Carson and his gift more than anyone ever has.

Lorelei Connor is a mother on the run. Her abusive ex-husband has followed her all over the country trying to steal their daughter. Distrusting of men and needing to keep on the move, she's surprised by her desire to remain close to Carson Alexander. Through her fear and hesitation, she must learn to rely on God to guide her—not an easy task when He's prompting her to trust a man. Can their relationship withstand the tragedy lurking on the horizon? Find out in **In His Sight** *Part of **Love in Season** collection of short stories*

* * *

Once again..... THANK YOU!

I pray you've been blessed as I have by your purchase of this book. If you've ***enjoyed Lori's Redemption*** please write a positive review and post it at online retailers (Amazon, B&N, Kobo, iBooks, etc.) and websites where readers gather and/or your social media platforms (FaceBook, Good Reads, BookBub, Twitter, etc).

Temperance Publishing

www.ingramcontent.com/pod-product-compliance
Lightning Source LLC
Chambersburg PA
CBHW011152190726

48288CB00010B/3288